CHAPTER ONE

"Charlotte, are you ready?" Rachel Walker stood on her front doorstep, waiting for her six-year-old daughter to come outside to head to school.

"Ready!" Charlotte ran up, backpack on, her blond hair tied back in one long braid.

While Rachel checked that her daughter had her lunch, snacks and the teddy bear she was taking in for show and tell, she said, "Remember to be careful at school, sweetie. Make sure your teachers know where you are all the time, and—"

Rachel's sister Emily, who was standing beside them on the front step, coughed pointedly. "Do we have to do this every morning? Charlotte is a big first-grader now and will be *fine.*"

Emily was thirty-two, only two years older than Rachel, but she always radiated a sense of confidence that Rachel never quite felt herself, despite the fact that they both shared the same

Walker genes—high cheekbones, deep blue eyes and golden-blond hair.

Emily smiled fondly at her niece. "Grandpa is waiting for us, so we should get going."

William Walker III, whom everyone called Tres, was sitting patiently behind the wheel of his car in front of the house. As one of the high school's English teachers, he'd only just returned from a school trip to Europe with his students one month ago when school started up again. It was good to have him back.

"All right, sweetie," Rachel said. "Give me a big hug and then go with Aunt Emily and your grandfather." They took Charlotte to school every day because it was just across the street from the high school where they both worked. Plus, Rachel knew that the three of them all loved having extra time together in the mornings.

Charlotte hugged her tight, the way she did every morning, then asked, "Do you think Grandpa will let me drive today? I know the way."

The fact that Charlotte was extremely precocious and always wanted to explore and try new things was yet another reason that Rachel was glad that Emily and their father were both so close to the elementary school. Even though they weren't in the same building as Charlotte, it was close enough that they could fairly easily keep an eye on her.

Rachel gave her daughter a smooch on the cheek. "One day, you'll definitely be able to drive yourself to school. But not until you're lots older."

WHEN IT'S LOVE

A Walker Island Romance, Book 3

Lucy Kevin

WHEN IT'S LOVE
A Walker Island Romance, Book 3
© 2015 Lucy Kevin

Once upon a time, Rachel Walker longed for—and sought out—adventure. But after her boyfriend found out she was pregnant and left her to raise her daughter Charlotte alone six years ago, she put her wild child days behind her. For good. So when Rachel's sister needs her to step in to help film a TV show with professional surfer Nicholas Quinn on Walker Island, she isn't the least bit worried about losing her heart to him. Not until the first time she sees him smile and realizes that her heart isn't completely closed off to promises of breathless excitement after all...

Nicholas has spent his entire life chasing adventure, one wave at a time, becoming a major surfing star along the way. But for all the incredible challenges he's faced around the world, he's never faced one as exciting—or as important—as winning Rachel's heart. One stolen kiss is all it takes for him to be absolutely certain that his next adventure should be taken with Rachel and her daughter Charlotte beside him. First, though, he'll have to break through every one of Rachel's walls to convince her to trust in both her dreams and his never-ending love.

"I'm almost six and a half now," Charlotte protested as Emily took her hand and walked with her out to the car. She climbed into the backseat, then waved out the window. "Bye, Mommy!"

Rachel waved back. "Have a great day at school, sweet girl!"

Thankfully, Charlotte was doing very well at school. Her teacher had said more than once during the past month that she was an absolutely wonderful addition to the first-grade class. It was everything that Rachel could have hoped for.

Even so, she was looking forward to Christmas break so that she could have her little girl at home with her again. Their house seemed far too empty without Charlotte there all day.

Rachel's phone rang as soon as she stepped back inside the house. It was Mr. Timmons, one of the partners at Timmons and Webb, the small insurance firm where she worked as an actuary. Despite being a small local firm they managed to do quite well, and when Rachel came back to the island a little more than six years ago, she'd been lucky to land a job with them. Calculating the financial impact of risk and uncertainty for a living might not be the most exciting job in the world, but the work was steady and dependable. Just the way she wanted—and needed— everything in her life to be for Charlotte.

"Good morning, Frank. Is everything okay at the office?"

"Just checking to see if you could come in this

afternoon rather than working at home for the full day? We're meeting with some potential new shipping clients after lunch, and I would very much like to have my best actuary go through the risk assessment."

"Sure, Frank, I'll be there at twelve thirty," she said, more than a little pleased to be called the "best" at something.

With four sisters, it wasn't always easy to stand out. Emily was so capable as she took care of the family home, along with doing such a great job as a high school counselor. Paige was always so elegant as she taught dance classes at the studio that their grandmother, Ava, owned. Morgan was a bigger TV star than ever now that her makeover program had hit it big. And Hanna was so creative and full of energy as she filmed both her documentaries and Morgan's show. Whereas Rachel was as normal as they came, simply trying to do her best to bring up her daughter as a single mother.

After she hung up the phone, Rachel began to work her way around the house, tidying up after the joyful chaos that was Charlotte. Six-year-olds were busy people, and there was no shortage of evidence that her little girl had been enjoying herself, both last night before bed and then again this morning before heading off to school.

Rachel smiled as she picked up a colorful drawing. Her profession might be as an actuary, but Charlotte was her real job. Being a mother was a full-time job, 24/7, and Rachel wouldn't trade that for anything in the world.

For a moment, she stood in the middle of the living room, just listening. It was so quiet in their small house with the view out over the bay, especially during the past month. It was hard to believe that her baby girl was growing up so fast. It felt like the last six years had passed in a flash. At this rate, in just the blink of an eye, Charlotte would be a teenager, dating boys, graduating...

"I think she gets to enjoy elementary school first," Rachel reminded herself. It wasn't as if her little girl was going to vanish from her life now that she was in first grade.

Rachel had often heard that it was a mother's job to worry. Well, if that was the case, she was more than qualified, considering that she could remember accident statistics the way her sister Hanna remembered Oscar nominees. As Charlotte got older, there would be boys to worry about, along with the rates of drunken driving among teenagers, not to mention the risks that would come if she and her friends started to hang out in the caves by the beach.

Again, Rachel forced these thoughts away as she went to hang up the drawing in Charlotte's bedroom, nearly tripping over the makeup kit her daughter had borrowed from Morgan the previous weekend. As far as she knew, her sister wasn't due on set to shoot an episode of her show today, and given that it had been nearly a week since she'd last seen her sister, Rachel decided to carve out a few minutes this morning to head over to Morgan's to return the kit.

The drive over to her sister's house wasn't far, but then nothing on Walker Island was too far away. That was one really nice thing about being back on the island—no matter how badly things had turned out with her ex, her family was always nearby.

The house Morgan shared with her fiancé, Brian, who taught science and coached football at the high school, had views out over the ocean and plenty of space for them to raise a family one day. Rachel loved to sit on her sister's front porch, staring out at that view and imagining all the places the ocean led to. The property also had a large garden where her sister spent much of her time. In fact, it was such a pretty day on the island that when Rachel pulled up to the gate and parked the car, she was a little surprised that Morgan wasn't out tending to the plants.

Rachel was about to knock on the front door when she heard Morgan coughing inside, hacking away as if she was about to bring up a lung.

"Morgan?" she called out. "It's Rachel. Are you okay?"

"Come in, Rachel," Morgan said a few moments later when she'd made it to the door. "It's not as bad as it soun—" Morgan started coughing again before she could finish her sentence.

Normally, her sister was a model of perfectly made-up beauty—her hair glossy, her makeup camera ready, her clothes the latest in fashion.

Today, however, she was wearing faded leggings and a T-shirt, her hair was a mess, and she wasn't wearing a stitch of makeup.

"Why didn't you tell me you were sick?" Rachel asked. After years of looking after Charlotte's colds and sniffles, she was quite good at dealing with them. "I could have picked up some medicine for you and brought over some chicken soup. You should be tucked up in bed, at the very least."

"I'm fine," Morgan insisted. "Really, I'm absolutely...whoa."

Rachel caught her sister as she staggered, then helped her back to the big couch in the living room. "Come on," she said in the same gentle voice that she used with Charlotte whenever her daughter wasn't feeling well. "Why don't you lie down, and I'll make you a cup of tea?"

"I'm just a little dizzy. It's nothing." Morgan clutched her temples. "All right, maybe it is pretty bad. But I can't afford to be sick. Not today." She looked up at Rachel with pleading eyes. "Is there any chance you could postpone heading into work for a bit to do a favor for me?"

"I'm not going in until after lunch, so whatever you need done, I'm sure I can take care of it for you with no problem at all."

Morgan coughed again, before saying, "I told you that Nicholas Quinn is coming out to the island, didn't I?"

"Yes, you said something about it on the weekend. He's a surfer, isn't he?"

"The best in the world, actually. The same people who produce my show want to do an extreme sports show with him as the host," Morgan explained. "The only problem is that he doesn't have any experience presenting or working in TV. So the idea is that he'll work with me and the production crew for a week or so to shoot some test segments for his show that will hopefully get the network on board. I'm supposed to meet him at the ferry"—her sister checked her watch—"in five minutes. Could you go pick him up and take him up to the house? It would be a total lifesaver."

"To the house? Isn't he staying at one of the hotels?" Because Walker Island had a thriving tourist trade and a large population of marine biologists and artists, it had plenty of hotels and small guesthouses.

"It was Grams' idea," Morgan explained. "When she heard that a colleague—and friend— of mine was coming, she insisted that she not only had plenty of space, but that a hotel was no way to get to know the real island. Nicholas is a great guy, so I figured he'd probably have fun with Grams and the rest of the gang. So can you go get him from the ferry?"

"Of course I'll go get him. And if you need anything else, call me right away."

Giving her a grateful smile, Morgan said, "Thank you so much, Rach. I'll text him right now to let him know you're on your way instead of me." A few seconds after sending the text, her eyes closed. She was already snoring by the time Rachel made it back to the front door and closed it behind her with a soft click.

* * *

Rachel made her way carefully over the winding roads of the island, never breaking the speed limit to get to the docks, though traffic was virtually nonexistent at this time of day. It was better to arrive safely and late than speed and possibly get into an accident.

From the magazines Morgan had left around the house while she was doing research on Nicholas, Rachel knew he had finely honed muscles, windswept blond hair and a couple of tattoos. Not to mention a gorgeous grin that had probably done more to get him this TV deal than anything else. His smile seemed so confident, so easy. A little too easy.

Or maybe it was just that Nicholas' carefree grin reminded her a little too much of another man with a similarly easy grin. One who had been quick to smile as long as things were fun, but who had walked away the moment things got serious. Because when Rachel had told Guy that she was pregnant with his child seven years ago, he hadn't even had the guts to say good-bye to her face. He'd simply hopped the next plane to Thailand and disappeared out of her—and her unborn child's—life forever.

No, you definitely couldn't trust a grin like that.

Bang!

The sound of her front right tire popping came a beat before the car went into a skid, swerving onto the dirt shoulder. Thankfully, she knew to steer into the skid, lightly touching the brakes until she was able to bring her car to a juddering halt by the side of the road. She sat there for a moment or two, letting the adrenaline fade, as much as it was likely to for the time being. Then she groaned. Having a flat meant the odds of making it to the docks by the time Nicholas' ferry arrived had gone from bad to nearly nonexistent. Unless, of course, she could do the world's fastest tire-changing job.

"There's no point in complaining," Rachel reminded herself aloud. "Just do the next sensible thing." She'd lived that motto for the past six years, knowing firsthand that no matter how hard things got, wishing things were different never changed a thing.

She got the spare out of the trunk along with the jack and the wrenches. One good thing about being cautious: It meant that she was generally prepared for those moments when something did go wrong. Rachel set about getting the jack into the special chassis socket, then began cranking the car up bit by bit. When she'd finished jacking up the car, she started work on taking the old wheel off so that she could switch it out for the spare. The nuts holding it in place were tighter than Rachel had anticipated, and the wrench scratched her palms as she worked them loose.

Finally, she wrestled the old wheel off, stowing it in the trunk before hoisting the spare into place and bolting it on.

The whole operation probably took ten minutes, and though she was pleased with how much easier the job had been than she'd expected, Rachel winced when she looked at herself in her car's rearview mirror.

How was it that grease and dirt always managed to get into places she was sure they hadn't touched? There was grease in her hair *and* on her cheeks, her clothes had tire tread marks on them, and her palms were red and chaffed from her efforts with the wrench.

In other words, she looked *horrible*. On the other hand, as a mother she was pretty used to being covered in paint or food or worse, so she supposed that by those standards a little grease was nothing.

Rachel got back on the road, heading toward the docks. Now that she was way behind schedule, it was incredibly tempting to go a little faster than the posted speed limit. Nothing major, just maybe take a few corners a little harder than she normally would have. That urge became almost overpowering when she found herself stuck behind a tractor. Rachel crawled along at a snail's pace, waiting for it to pull over to let her pass. Mere minutes seemed like hours now that she was officially fifteen minutes late.

She was considering the idea of pulling out into the oncoming lane and passing when, suddenly, a car zipped past going in the opposite direction. What if she had pulled out just then? And what if she'd been going faster when her tire blew out? What would happen to Charlotte if something happened to her?

It was the perfect reminder to Rachel not to take unnecessary risks just so she could gain a little time.

Finally, the tractor pulled into a field, and she was able to get past, making pretty good time for the rest of the journey to the ferry terminal. As she pulled into the parking lot, she sent up a silent prayer that she wouldn't bump into anyone she knew. Between the grease and the dirt, she definitely wasn't looking her best.

She soon spotted Nicholas at the end of the jetty, and her stomach immediately knotted up. He had looked impressive enough on magazine covers, but seeing him in the flesh?

Oh my...he was *gorgeous*!

Nicholas had a couple of bags at his feet, and he was holding on to a surfboard. There was a small crowd of onlookers around him, people who had clearly been caught up by his charisma. As Rachel began to make her way over, she realized Nicholas was telling his adoring crowd a story.

"So there I was, I'd lost sight of land and I wasn't sure which way I was supposed to be heading. All of a sudden, this crew of oceanographers shows up, and we get to talking about the waves over on the next island, so I end up taking a ride out with them to go check them out. Only, when I get back, I find out that half the Coast Guard was out looking for me, thinking that I'd drowned."

His hands were animated as he talked, and he flashed that easygoing smile at the crowd around him as they hung on his every word. The ocean breeze picked up a little, ruffling his hair and lifting up his shirt just enough for Rachel to see a hint of perfect washboard abs.

Not that she was purposely looking, of course. After all, he was clearly an adventure-seeking show-off who'd never grown up. After Guy, she was all too familiar with guys like him, and they were definitely not her type anymore. In fact, the whole image Nicholas presented to the world left her cold.

At least, it *should* have left her cold and disinterested. Instead, she couldn't seem to stop hanging on his every word, while trying not to think about just how messy and untidy she must look.

Of course, it was right when she was trying to run a surreptitious hand through her hair that he looked straight at her and smiled. A smile that made him look even *more* perfect, darn it.

CHAPTER TWO

Nicholas had always been told that he could surf before he could walk, since one of his uncles used to hold him on a board in the very shallowest water when he was just a few months old. Honestly, he couldn't remember a time when he *hadn't* been surfing. Growing up in Hawaii, that wasn't so unusual, given that swimming and surfing were things that nearly every Hawaiian did. Nicholas was only exceptional inasmuch as he surfed professionally, did occasional stunt work, and generally found ways to keep life exciting wherever he went. There were so many things in the world that allowed him to get his adrenaline pumping by pushing himself a little further every day...and he loved it.

Even coming to this little island in the Pacific Northwest was an adventure. Places like Walker Island tended to bring out the drive in people to try to be so much more. Just like it had with

Morgan Walker—she'd grown up here and had become a huge success with both her locally grown organic makeup line and now her TV show as well.

Walker Island was twenty degrees cooler than Hawaii, and the waves were much smaller, but as far as he could tell from chatting with some locals on the ferry ride over, it had the same close-knit community feel to it. And, just like in Hawaii, he bet people here spent as much time outdoors as they did inside.

"What is your first impression of our island from the ferry?" one of the people on board had asked him after they'd recognized him sitting on deck with his surfboard.

"It reminds me of home. There's nothing as good as island life." He spent much of his time traveling to all corners of the world, but he always loved being on an island best.

"What's the best wave you've ever ridden?" someone else had asked. "Was it that one you caught at Mavericks this year?"

If there was one thing that Nicholas took seriously, it was waves. Which was why he'd brought his board to Walker Island despite the fact that it was not a well-known surfing destination. He wanted to be ready if it turned out that the perfect wave was just around the corner.

"The best wave so far this year was one I caught not far from my house in Hawaii," Nicholas had replied. "I was out surfing with some buddies, and there it was. The right height, the right curl, everything. The conditions hadn't even been all that great until then, and it reminded me of what life is all about—if I only put myself out there when things seem to be perfect, I'll miss out on the times when they unexpectedly *are* perfect. It was great the way it all worked out."

"Will you actually be trying to surf around Walker Island?"

Nicholas smiled. "Like I said, I'm always searching for that perfect wave. And you never know where—or when—it will show up."

Nicholas turned then to look out over the crowd for his ride...and saw what looked very much like the perfect woman. There was no other way to describe her. She was blond-haired, beautiful in a way that made it almost impossible for Nicholas to look anywhere else, and best of all, she was coming straight toward him.

As he'd just said, you never knew when perfection would show up.

Morgan had texted to let him know that her sister Rachel was going to be picking him up from the ferry, and he could easily see the family resemblance. Looked like it was his lucky day.

"I've got to go, guys," Nicholas said to the fans who had gathered around. "I'm pretty sure my ride is here."

As he moved closer to her, he noted that she had grease on her face and in her hair. "Hi, I'm Nicholas."

He wanted to reach out and wipe away the

grease on her cheek with the pad of his thumb. Partly because he didn't like the idea of anything marring her beauty. Mostly, though, he just wanted the excuse to touch her. He stopped himself, though, because he always liked to take his time when it came to women. He didn't want to rush things when he could savor them. "You must be Morgan's sister Rachel. Thank you for coming to get me."

For a moment or two, she didn't say anything, simply stared back at him with eyes bluer than even the bluest ocean waters. Her gaze, however, was slightly wary, and he immediately wanted to know why.

"Sorry I'm late," she finally said. "I had a little tire trouble on the way here."

Morgan had told Nicholas all about her four sisters, saying he would need that much information to survive staying at the family house with her grandmother and sisters. But she hadn't told him that he was going to fall head over heels for Rachel from nothing more than one glance—and a few softly spoken words.

"Ah, so that's why you've got grease on your cheek." This time, Nicholas did reach out to wipe it away, forgetting whether or not it was too soon to make a move like this. "Is everything all right now?"

That first touch of her skin against his was electric, just as he'd known it would be. But instead of moving closer, she took a step back before saying, "Everything's fine."

From the way she said it, a little too fast and slightly breathless, he guessed that she'd felt the sparks jump just as much as he had from the one simple touch.

"I've left my car down by the next jetty, so we'll have to walk over there. I know my grandmother is looking forward to seeing you up at the house, and my sisters Emily and Paige will be there later today, too."

"And you?" Nicholas asked hopefully.

"I have my own place for just me and Charlotte, my little girl."

He remembered that Morgan had told him Rachel was a single mother and that she was doing a really great job of raising her daughter. "It must be nice to have that big family of yours nearby."

"It is, most of the time."

"When your sister isn't having you pick up strange guys from the docks?" Nicholas suggested with a smile.

"Something like that." He thought he saw her lips twitch before she said, "We'd better get going. Grams will be expecting you, and Morgan will want to know that you got to the isla—"

Rachel stopped as her phone rang. She answered, and Nicholas could see the concern on her face when she looked at the number on the screen and picked up. "Yes, this is Rachel Walker. Oh no, she is? She seemed fine this morning, although her aunt isn't very well either. Yes, I'll be right there. I'm at the ferry terminal, so it will be less than ten minutes."

As she slipped her phone back into her pocket, Rachel looked over at him. "It's Charlotte. She's sick, and I have to go pick her up at school immediately. Which means we're really going to have to hurry so that I can drop you off at Grams' place on the way."

"There's no need to do that," Nicholas said. It was obvious how much Rachel wanted to get to her daughter, and he couldn't stand the thought of a sick little girl shivering in the school office as she waited for her mother to come get her. "Just take me along with you."

"Take you with me?" She looked more than a little stunned by his suggestion. "I'm sure you don't want to be around a sick child."

"Why not?" He'd already decided that he would take more time with Rachel any way he could get it. "Especially if it will work out better for you to head straight there."

Apart from her little girl getting sick, it seemed that everything really *was* working out. He'd already had a great ferry ride over to the island, seen a couple of whales, met the most beautiful woman on the island, and now he was getting to spend more time in her company. What could be better than that?

Though she was still clearly surprised by his offer to go pick up her daughter together, a moment later she finally smiled and said, "Thank you, I really appreciate it."

Nicholas had seen many beautiful things in his travels, but he'd never seen anything as pretty as Rachel's smile.

CHAPTER THREE

Nicholas quickly tied the surfboard into place on the roof of Rachel's car with some bungee cords and rope that he pulled out of his bag. While he worked, she thought about all the places he must have been with this surfboard. Hawaii, Brazil and hundreds of beaches around the world. Places she'd always wanted to go...but once she had Charlotte, traveling to new places, and seeking out new adventures, wasn't at the top of her list anymore. Not even close.

"That should be secure enough," he said as he finally stepped back from the car. "I know you're anxious to pick up your daughter."

"How quickly can I drive without worrying that it will slide off?"

"We should be just fine. Unless you're planning on doing some white-knuckle stunt driving," he teased.

Rachel was surprised that he would even

suggest that about her. Didn't he see what everyone else did? The staid and steady single mom. The woman who did the right thing—the *safe* thing—all the time.

Or was it possible that he could see the glimmer of the girl she used to be? Wild...and more than a little unruly and adventurous.

Shaking off her thoughts of the past, she got into the car and buckled up, waiting until Nicholas did the same before setting off through town.

As they made their way up along one of the winding roads, Nicholas said, "Walker Island looks like a really great place."

"It's a fairly quiet island," she said, already distracted enough by trying to concentrate on the road rather than on the gorgeous profile of the man sitting next to her without trying to make sparkling conversation, too. Did Nicholas *have* to go around being that good-looking? Rachel knew all too well just how many accidents were caused every year by distracted driving.

"Something tells me," he replied in a deep voice that made her more than a little melty in all the places she hadn't so much as felt *warm* these past few years, "that things will be exciting enough for me here, even if I don't parachute out of a helicopter the way one of the TV producers was suggesting."

"Are you really thinking of doing that?" Just thinking of what it would be like to jump out of a helicopter over the island with a parachute on her back sent a rush of adrenaline through Rachel.

"Actually, I was planning to stick to aquatic pursuits, but now that you mention it, that would probably be one heck of a way to get a great aerial view of the island." She could feel him turn his gaze to her from the passenger seat. "I'm glad the school is close by so that you can get to your daughter soon."

"Sometimes the island feels too small," she found herself telling him, "but on days like today, it's definitely a good thing." Rachel wouldn't be able to relax until she'd made certain that Charlotte's illness was just the bug the teachers thought it was.

They pulled into the school parking lot sixty seconds later, and after Rachel let Nicholas know she'd be right back, she rushed in to find the school nurse who had Charlotte in her office. The poor little thing looked practically green as she sat there, and when Rachel reached out to touch her forehead, it felt burning hot.

"I'm sure it isn't anything to worry about," the nurse assured Rachel. "Lots of kids have been coming down with the flu. Charlotte will just have to stay home from school for a day or two, I'd expect."

"Thank you," Rachel said, lifting Charlotte up to carry her, wanting the feeling of her daughter in her arms, knowing she was safe. "I'll get her to the doctor right now."

Charlotte's eyes grew big as they approached

the car. "Mommy, why is there a surfboard on top of the car?"

"A friend of Morgan's is in town, and I went to pick him up at the ferry. It's his surfboard."

"Do you think he could teach me to surf?"

Rachel's chest tightened. Charlotte had always been a little adventurer, and it wasn't always easy for Rachel to walk the fine line between keeping her daughter safe and giving her wings to fly.

"I don't know, sweetheart. But right now, we've got to take you to the doctor and get you well." When Charlotte didn't argue about going to see the doctor, Rachel realized just how bad she must be feeling.

As Rachel got her daughter buckled into her car seat in the back of the car, Charlotte asked Nicholas, "Are you the surfer?"

Nicholas grinned at her. "That's me. My name is Nicholas, and you must be Charlotte."

"That's me," her daughter echoed with a smile that temporarily seemed to take away her pallor. "Is surfing fun?"

His grin grew even wider. "Some of the most fun I've ever had."

"What happens if you fall off?"

"Then I just swim out and try again."

"I bet *I* wouldn't fall off."

"Everyone falls off. That's half the fun."

Despite how easily Nicholas was chatting with her daughter while they drove, from the rearview mirror Rachel could see Charlotte's skin grow even more flushed. The island's busy doctor's office was the only one in the small community, which meant that they had to cope with everything from tourists who felt a little sick to serious maritime accidents.

Charlotte's eyes were closed by the time Rachel pulled up outside the doctor's office. Quickly lifting her daughter out of the car, she was surprised when Charlotte said to Nicholas, "Aren't you coming with us?"

He smiled at her. "As long as it's okay with your mommy."

Rachel didn't know what to make of her daughter's fascination with Nicholas. Or, rather, she *wished* she didn't know what to make of it. The problem was that she was very much afraid she and Charlotte were two peas in a pod where the good-looking surfer was concerned.

"That's fine with me, unless you're worried that someone will make off with your board."

"It seems a little quiet here for that," Nicholas said before turning his smile to her daughter again. "Let's go in so that you can start feeling all better."

With Charlotte in her arms, Rachel hurried into the waiting room and explained things to the receptionist. While she completed several forms, Nicholas was nice enough to keep her daughter company in the waiting room. Charlotte still looked quite ill, but she was obviously enjoying telling him about the art project they'd been working on in class before she got sick. Rachel hoped her daughter didn't end up infecting him. She could only imagine how upset the TV network would be if Nicholas was laid up in bed when he should be filming.

Ten minutes later, she and Charlotte went through to see the doctor, who checked her temperature, throat and ears and proclaimed it to be the flu that was going around the island.

"Just like that?" Rachel asked. "Shouldn't you do a few more in-depth tests first?"

"I could, Ms. Walker, but honestly, I've seen so many cases of this in the last few days that there really isn't any need. I'm sure we wouldn't want to distress Charlotte by doing tests she doesn't need."

Charlotte buried her head against Rachel's chest at the word "tests." She obviously didn't like that idea. Even so, there was a part of Rachel that wanted to overrule them both and insist that the doctor make absolutely certain it wasn't anything more serious.

Perhaps the doctor guessed what she was thinking—and how much she worried about anything ever happening to her daughter—because he said, "Why don't I give you a prescription for some children's medicine that will help alleviate the symptoms and make it easier for Charlotte to sleep? But honestly, in this situation, what she mostly needs is rest. If she isn't feeling better in a couple of days, or if her symptoms get worse, bring her back right away."

Rachel nodded. She knew she should be

relieved that it was as simple as that, but she couldn't help but worry all the same. As she went out into the waiting area with Charlotte, she saw that Nicholas had yet again attracted a small crowd of people who couldn't get enough of his surfing stories.

From Rachel's arms, Charlotte looked around at the crowd and then at Nicholas, who immediately excused himself from his group of admirers when he saw them.

"Are you famous?" Charlotte asked him.

Nicholas shrugged. "Maybe a little bit."

"My Aunt Morgan is famous, too. She's on TV."

When Charlotte put her head down on Rachel's shoulder and closed her eyes again, Nicholas lowered his voice and asked, "How's she doing?"

"The doctor says she'll be fine in a day or two, although he did give us a prescription for some medicine to help her sleep better. Grams' house isn't far from ours, so if it's okay with you, we'll make one more stop to pick up Charlotte's medicine at the pharmacy and then I'll drop you off on the way home."

"Whatever you need works for me," Nicholas assured her.

What Rachel needed right then was to get home with her daughter. That, and figure out what she was going to do about work that afternoon. Morgan was still sick, obviously. Emily and their father were both at work. Paige would be busy teaching classes down at the studio. That left either Grams or Rachel's honorary stepbrother, Michael. She sighed, thinking that the hardest thing about being a single parent was having to come up with contingency plans for someone else to watch Charlotte. Every instinct she had made her want to be right there at home with her daughter, ready to comfort her if she needed it.

Rachel put Charlotte into her car seat and, to her surprise, Nicholas got into the back beside her. "So I can keep an eye on her while you're driving home," he explained.

As it turned out, it mostly gave Charlotte someone to talk to as she perked back up a little again. She told him all about how she was practicing a butterfly dance up at the dance studio this week. Then she insisted on playing *I Spy* with Nicholas, who didn't seem to mind that half the things Charlotte guessed had gone past before he could look out for them.

The three of them made quick work getting the prescription from the pharmacy, but as soon as they were back in the car and finally on the way to Rachel's grandmother's house, Charlotte suddenly turned away from Nicholas.

"Mommy, I don't feel well."

"It's okay, sweetie, we'll be home in a minute."

"No, Mommy, I feel like I'm going to—"

There was no time to pull over and get her out of the car. No time to even shout a warning to

Nicholas. One moment, Charlotte was sitting there chatting with Nicholas as happy as she had been all day.

The next, she was busy throwing up all over Nicholas' shirt.

CHAPTER FOUR

Rachel was horrified. Her baby had just thrown up all over Nicholas! He was used to glamor and glitz, exotic locations and pristine beaches, not small children making a complete mess of his shirt.

She looked back to the road just in time to brake as a couple of teenagers crossed in front of her, bringing the car to a stop with a jolt that sent the surfboard skidding halfway down the windshield, even though Nicholas had tied it on so well.

Rachel pulled over to the side of the road, but instead of getting out to deal with his surfboard, Nicholas continued to try to soothe Charlotte, who was crying now.

"I've got her," Rachel said softly as she grabbed some tissues from her purse to clean up the worst of it. "Maybe you could work on the surfboard," she suggested to Nicholas. After another concerned glance at Charlotte, he finally nodded and got out of the car.

What else could go wrong today? Rachel wondered as she worked to persuade her daughter to take at least a small drink from a bottle of water she'd had in the car. But when she finally stopped crying and her eyes closed, Rachel decided it would be better to let her rest for the time being.

A few seconds later, she stepped out from the backseat to see if Nicholas needed any help with the surfboard...and nearly gasped out loud when she realized that he had pulled off his soiled shirt and the planes of his chest and abs were now on full display. His physique wasn't massive like a body builder's, rather it was well defined and perfectly balanced—and she *really* needed to stop staring at him like a teenage girl with a crush!

"I am *so* sorry about that. I should have guessed that she might get sick in the car and made sure you weren't sitting next to her just in case it did happen."

"Don't worry about it. I've had plenty of worse things happen to me while traveling around the world."

"You've been so nice about everything today," she said softly. "Thank you."

"You're the one who was nice enough to come get me from the ferry. There's nothing to thank me for."

But there was, because Charlotte's own father had never done as much for his daughter as Nicholas already had today. In fact, Guy had never even *seen* his daughter, let alone tried to soothe her while she was sick.

It was very kind of Nicholas to brush off the accident as nothing. Not everyone would have done that. After years of motherhood, Rachel knew her clothes never stayed clean for very long with her daughter around, yet even her sister Morgan was still learning not to wear her more expensive designer clothes around her little niece. Of course, Nicholas was currently managing without his shirt completely, wearing only a single shark tooth on a leather thong around his neck.

She had to hand it to him—he was certainly taking all this better than any man could or should have. Instead of shouting at her or demanding that she replace the shirt, he was being totally calm, and kind, about the whole thing.

The few men she'd dated since Guy had always run a mile the moment they found out she had a child. That, or they'd treated her daughter like an annoyance, thinking it was odd that Rachel would want to spend so much of her time with her little girl.

But why was she thinking about how the men she'd dated had treated her daughter when it simply wasn't relevant in this situation? Even if the heat that rose inside of Rachel every time Nicholas looked at her insisted otherwise.

She was simply giving him a ride to help out

her sister, she reminded herself. That was it. She would drop him off at her grandmother's house soon and then she probably wouldn't see him again. Granted, he would be on the island for the next week, but he'd be busy doing his TV thing with Morgan.

"If it's okay, I'd like to get Charlotte into bed and then help get you cleaned up." At his slightly curious look, she explained, "I can't have you showing up at Grams' house like this. Morgan would never forgive me. Besides, the least I owe you is a shower."

"A shower would be great, thanks."

Getting back into the car, with Nicholas in the backseat again as he insisted on keeping watch over Charlotte, she hurried back through the streets of Walker Island's small community, hoping with every turn she took that the surfboard wouldn't go flying off the top of the car.

Finally, she pulled up in front of her house, plucking Charlotte from the backseat and carrying her inside with Nicholas following behind. "If you'll wait a few minutes for me to get Charlotte into bed, I can show you where everything is."

"I'm sure I can find the shower just fine if you'll point me in the general direction. And I have plenty of spare clothes in my bag."

Pity, she thought before she could stop her brain from going in that direction. "Great!" Her smile was brighter than it needed to be on account of the heated thoughts she was working to corral—and conceal. The problem was, she was fairly certain he knew *exactly* what she had been thinking. "The shower's just down the hall, and there are towels under the sink."

Rachel carried Charlotte through their small house to her bedroom. Their place was compact, furnished in things they'd managed to buy secondhand or that had been handed down from her grandmother and sisters. Rachel had taken a lot of care when it came to decorating her daughter's room and the whole family had helped paint it, which was lovely of them.

While she set about cleaning up Charlotte and getting her ready for bed, she could hear her shower running. It was hard not to imagine Nicholas in the bathroom, steam rising around him...

Rachel cut the thought off, the same way that she usually made herself dismiss thoughts about exotic locales and long-distance trips, knowing she needed to focus on the practical realities of her life instead. She dressed Charlotte in her pajamas, settled her under the covers, then gently woke her up to give her a capful of the medicine she'd picked up from the pharmacy. Even drowsy, Charlotte made a face as she drank it.

"I wish it tasted nicer, too," Rachel said gently, "but I promise it will make you feel better."

As she reached down to wipe Charlotte's brow, her daughter shut her eyes again. Hopefully, she would be fine soon, just the way the doctor said. Still, Rachel couldn't bear to leave her—not even with Grams—today. Which meant she had a couple of phone calls to make.

She decided to try her boss first. Frank's secretary put her through after a few seconds.

"Hi, Rachel, are you going to be in soon?"

"Actually, that's what I need to talk to you about."

"Oh no. Rachel, don't do this to me. We have the salvage people coming in—"

"Charlotte's ill. I've had to bring her home from school because she's been throwing up and has a fever." Before Frank could protest, she quickly suggested, "Why don't you send me over everything you have and I'll come up with the figures from home? In fact, we could do a conference call or share screens online later if you'd like."

"You're not sick, too, are you?" Frank asked, obviously concerned about how long that would keep her off work.

"No, but my sister Morgan has come down with the same thing, so it's obviously pretty contagious."

"You're right," he quickly agreed upon hearing the word 'contagious'. "You should stay home today. I'll send over their details as soon as I can."

"And I'll get to work on the risk calculations immediately. I'm sure they'll be quite complicated, but hopefully I'll be able to give you a draft inside of two days." Which was at least a full day faster than she normally would take on a project of this size. But even if it meant working through the night, she'd make it happen. Rachel had learned early on after having Charlotte that she could juggle just about anything in her life, so long as she didn't mind going without sleep.

She hung up and checked on her daughter. Charlotte seemed a little restless, murmuring in her sleep, but at least her skin felt cooler to the touch. Rachel tiptoed out of the room to make her next phone call—to Michael.

When he answered on the second ring, she immediately said, "I'm so sorry to call you in the middle of your workday like this, but Morgan sent me down to the docks to collect Nicholas Quinn, a surfer who's going to be shadowing her for the week for a TV show he's filming, and then Charlotte got sick so I had to pick her up at school, and now that she's napping I have to stay here with her, which means that I can't bring him over to Grams' house the way I promised Morgan that I would."

Fortunately, Michael had lived with Rachel and her sisters for several years as a teenager, so he could follow her long and winding sentence fairly easily. "Do you need me to go down to the ferry terminal?"

"No, to my house. Charlotte got sick *after* I picked him up, so Nicholas is here."

"Don't worry about a thing. I'll be right over," Michael said.

Feeling immensely grateful to the man who

had always been there for her and her sisters—even now that they were all grown up—Rachel took another quick glance at Charlotte before heading through the house in search of Nicholas since the shower was no longer running. She should let him know that Michael was coming to collect him, maybe give him a hand getting his surfboard off the roof of her car, too. Maybe he was down in the kitchen, getting a glass of water or...

"Oh!" Rachel exclaimed as she almost collided with Nicholas, who was coming out of the bathroom.

He wasn't wearing anything except for the towel wrapped around his waist. It shouldn't have been that different from seeing him without his shirt as they'd checked on the surfboard earlier. But somehow it was.

Very different.

Barely able to form a coherent thought, all she could manage was, "Where are your clothes?"

"I forgot to bring them in here with me, and I knew you were putting Charlotte to bed, so I figured I had a pretty clear run to my bags and my clothes. It was this or put my old ones back on, which would kind of defeat the purpose of the shower, right?"

"Right," Rachel agreed reluctantly.

She knew better, knew she shouldn't be staring, but she was only human...and she knew with utter certainty that there wasn't a female alive who wouldn't have looked right then. The muscles of Nicholas' torso were strongly defined from swimming through strong waves all day. He was still wearing the shark tooth around his neck, and this close, Rachel could make out the details of the swirling, almost tribal-style tattoos on his skin, along with a few scars that she guessed were mementos of moments when a surfing experience had gone sideways. They should have marred the smooth planes of his chest and abs, particularly since they were obviously signs of what a risk-taker the man in front of her could be. But, somehow, they only seemed to make him sexier.

When Rachel finally looked up again, he was grinning. A ridiculously gorgeous grin this time, one that made her fingers itch to touch him and her lips tingle with the desire to kiss him. They were staring into each other's eyes, all of the heady possibilities swirling between them, when the doorbell rang and immediately yanked Rachel right out of the spell Nicholas had put over her.

Michael was here to take the surfer off her hands...just in time to save her from doing something she would regret.

CHAPTER FIVE

As Rachel went to answer the doorbell, Nicholas quickly dug a pair of jeans and a shirt out of his bag. After he finished dressing and walked back toward the kitchen, he could hear her saying, "Thanks so much for dropping everything to come take Morgan's guest to Grams, Michael. Between getting a flat tire on the way to the ferry, the call from Charlotte's school, and then her throwing up all over him in the backseat of the car, somehow it turned into this epic odyssey."

Nicholas heard Michael laugh, then say, "She threw up on him?"

"Don't laugh," she replied, although he could hear humor seep into her voice. "It was so nice of him to offer to hang out in the backseat with her to try to keep her spirits up. And then *splat!* Poor guy, it was really gross. I'm sure he's dying to get out of here and into Grams' house by now."

But she was wrong about that—and he'd be shocked if she didn't know by now that he wasn't at all in a hurry to get away from her or her daughter, even if it meant risking getting splashed by Charlotte again.

In any case, Nicholas felt a little weird listening in on their conversation. It felt as if he was intruding on a private family affair. He knew how families worked, although he didn't really have much of one to call his own anymore and was starting to realize just how much he missed it. Quite a bit, actually.

How close were Rachel and this Michael guy, he wondered. Close enough that she could call on him at a moment's notice, obviously. And Nicholas knew that he couldn't be the only one who saw what a beautiful, interesting woman she was.

"Speaking of getting out of the house, once Charlotte's all better, if you'd like me to take her out to see a movie one night so that you can—"

"Look, here's Nicholas," Rachel said, cutting Michael off before he could say exactly what Rachel would be doing on a night without her daughter—although it wasn't a stretch at all for Nicholas to assume it was likely a hot date with some guy who would spend all night drooling over how gorgeous she was.

Michael looked to be a couple of years older than Rachel, with the muscular physique of someone who worked with his hands. Nicholas could see the other man giving him the same appraisal.

"Hi, I'm Nicholas."

"Michael." The other man's grip was firm and a bit rough. "Rachel asked me to come give you a ride over to Grams'."

"Thanks." Nicholas turned to Rachel. "And thank you for bringing me this far. I hope I'll see more of you when Charlotte's feeling better."

She looked a little flustered at that and sounded just as flustered as she said, "I...you..." She shook her head as if to clear it. "I'm sure I'll see you up at Grams' house."

Nicholas went and untied his surfboard from the roof of Rachel's car then attached it to the roof rack on Michael's SUV. Michael seemed like a nice enough guy, and even better, Nicholas hadn't noticed any sparks jumping between him and Rachel. Still, he needed to know for sure.

"So, you and Rachel, are you..." Nicholas said as Michael pulled out onto the road.

Michael looked more than a little shocked at the idea, which immediately put Nicholas' mind at ease. "The Walkers took me in when I was a teenager," he explained. "Rachel and I are like brother and sister." That came with a slightly pointed look. One that clearly said Michael considered them his family and that Nicholas should be respectful and not cause them any problems.

"Rachel is one of five, isn't she?" Morgan had given him the rundown on her sisters, but after he'd met—and been so stunned by—Rachel, the details on the other Walker women had gone a bit fuzzy in his head.

"I'll give you a quick rundown of everyone before we get to the house," Michael said. "You're staying with Ava, their grandmother. She's a lot of fun. Used to be a dancer over in Seattle. Tres, that's William Walker III, is their father. You probably won't see that much of him, because he doesn't come up to the house much. Then there are the Walker sisters. Hanna is the youngest. She's a filmmaker. Next is Morgan, who you know. After Morgan, there's Paige. You'll probably meet her up at the house if she isn't at the dance studio teaching classes or getting students ready for their next performance. Rachel's the second-oldest, and then there's Emily. She's a guidance counselor at the school and also runs things around the house." His voice softened when he talked about Emily, especially as he said, "She's pretty special."

"Are they all going to be okay with me staying up at the family house?" Nicholas asked. He'd been surprised when Morgan had insisted that he stay with her grandmother. Surprised and maybe a little worried about ruining a collection of lace doilies, or that Ava might turn out to own a dozen cats. Now, though, it sounded more like he had to worry about not upsetting a whole bevy of sisters.

"It's just Emily, Paige and Grams up at the house. Morgan, Hanna and Rachel all have their own places. Besides, Ava's the one who insisted that you come and stay. Depending on how busy things are with the dance studio, Paige might not even notice you're there."

"So, if Emily runs the place, is there any way of making sure I stay on her good side while I'm here?"

"I've yet to find a way of doing that—a way that works, anyway," Michael said, although there was something almost possessive about the way he said it. Almost as if he was trying to suss out whether Nicholas was planning to make a move on Emily. "Although that could just be me. She and I have always had a different relationship from the others. We both like to be handy and in charge—so it means we butt heads quite a bit."

Nicholas had never been very good at going along with other's plans either. He'd always been more about doing what felt right, regardless of who was telling him to do otherwise. It was one of the reasons he was looking forward to doing this TV work. He'd been surfing competitively for so long that he was interested in trying new things just for the joy of them, rather than because of a need to win a prize.

"I'll try not to cause any problems," Nicholas promised just as they pulled up to the curb.

The house he'd be staying in for the next week was a big, old-fashioned place, obviously built many years ago, with plenty of space for a large family, but obviously well cared for.

Michael led the way inside, letting himself in with the ease of a man who obviously felt right at home. He took the bags into the hall while Nicholas carried his surfboard.

A spritely older woman stepped into the hallway. She was elegantly dressed in a long skirt and a pale blue blouse, and she moved with the grace of an athlete. Her features were beautiful and full of character. Nicholas could easily see the resemblance to Rachel.

She took his hand in a firm grip. "You must be Nicholas. I'm Ava. It's lovely to have you here. Why don't you leave your things here for now and come through to the kitchen? You can prop your surfboard against the stairs."

Nicholas followed her into the kitchen, where she began to make coffee, waving away Michael's attempt to help. "If you really want to help, you can tell me why my social network accounts all seem to be going wrong at once."

"More computer troubles?" Michael went over to a big, family-sized kitchen table and started tapping away on a laptop.

"You're a professional surfer, aren't you?" Ava said. "That must be a lot of fun. I tried surfing a couple of times when I was younger, but Walker Island doesn't really have the waves for it."

Nicholas wasn't sure whether she was serious or not, but he did know that he hadn't met that many grandmothers with quite so much life in them as this one. He liked her a great deal already and knew he was going to have a great time staying in her home.

"The guest bedroom we've made up for you is

just upstairs. You won't have trouble finding it."

"It's a great house," Nicholas said. "I'll bet a lot of great memories were made here."

She smiled at him then, a smile that reminded him of the one Rachel had given him. "You're right about that. So many wonderful memories. With more being made all the time." She handed him a cup of coffee. "Emily and Paige are at work at the moment, but I'm sure they'll be home for dinner. Paige helps me run my dance school. I think you'll like her when you meet her. All that training and athleticism—you're bound to have a lot in common. And Emily is probably finishing up a meeting with one of her students about which university they'd like to attend in the fall."

Was Ava trying to set him up with one of her granddaughters? If so, she was choosing the wrong sisters. There was only one of her five granddaughters that Nicholas was interested in knowing more about.

"Tell me more about Rachel."

"Rachel?"

"Morgan asked her to give me a ride over from the ferry, and we were en route when Charlotte got sick at school, so we went by to pick her up and took her over to the doctor together and then immediately home to bed. Michael brought me over from Rachel's house."

"Charlotte's such a lovely little girl," Ava said, a frown marring her brow. "I so hate it when she doesn't feel well. I'll have to call over there—"

He put a hand on her arm in hopes of calming

her worries. "The doctor said Charlotte has the flu that's been going around and will hopefully be better in just a couple of days."

"I hope so. Rachel is such a good mother, and I know how hard it is for her that there's little she can do to help her little girl until the bug runs its course."

Ava was right about Rachel and Charlotte. They had an amazing mother-daughter dynamic, one that was sweet and pure. As an adult, Nicholas had been so busy flying around the world to surf that none of his relationships had lasted very long. Yet, spending time with the two of them today had shown him exactly what was missing from his own life: family.

"Thank you for the hospitality, and the coffee, Ava. I'll take my bags up to my room and get out of your way for a while."

"I'll help find a better place to store that surfboard," Michael offered as he followed him into the hall.

Nicholas didn't really need the help, but he was grateful for the opportunity to ask Michael another question. "Is Rachel seeing anyone right now?"

"No," Michael said with a shake of his head. "She doesn't really date, and she's probably not even your type anyway. I mean, you're a professional daredevil, right?" He didn't wait for Nicholas to reply before saying, "She's all about playing things safe. I seriously doubt she'd be interested."

Playing things safe. Funny, Nicholas hadn't seen her like that. Careful with her daughter, of course, but there'd been fire in her eyes more than once in the short time he'd spent with her.

"I'll leave you to get settled in," Michael said as he headed off with the surfboard.

It didn't take Nicholas long to unpack. He was, after all, used to life on the road. After getting organized, he headed out onto the upstairs landing toward the stairs, but when he passed by an open door and realized that it was Rachel's old room, he couldn't help but want to take a closer look.

There were dozens of pictures of her and her friends and family stuck around a floor-length mirror, and none of them fit with the idea of *playing things safe.* She was rock-climbing in one picture, water-skiing in another. A third had been taken from what was obviously the limb of a very tall tree. In each of them, Rachel was smiling, obviously enjoying the excitement of it all. The same man was beside her in most of the shots and "Rachel and Guy" was written on the bottom of one of the pictures.

At the very center of the photo collage was a page torn from a high school yearbook. *Most Likely To Have Fun* was the caption and Rachel's features stared back at him, happy and beautiful as the ocean breeze blew through her blond hair and waves crashed over her bare feet.

CHAPTER SIX

Amazingly, the following morning Charlotte looked as right as rain and really wanted to go to school. Immediately after Emily and Rachel's father came to pick Charlotte up to take her to school, Rachel headed into the small insurance office on the island to try to finish up the risk assessments she'd promised her boss.

The reports for the salvage crews were every bit as complex as she'd thought they would be. Along with the usual issues that came with shipping—from the state and model of the individual ships to the knowledge the captains had of the waters in the area—there were the risks associated with diving and the recovery of material from the ocean bed. Basically, the salvage crews were making massive bets on finding treasure at the bottom of the ocean. All of which contributed to high premiums, but exactly how high? Rachel had been working on the math for most of last night and today, as well, but every time she finally started to get a grip on it, it felt as if the numbers kept slipping away.

"How is the report coming, Rachel?" Frank asked, putting his balding head around the door. "Will you have it for me by the end of the day?"

"Absolutely, Frank," Rachel promised.

The truth was that if she'd been able to think straight, she might have already had it done. But every time she tried to focus, the image of Nicholas wrapped in nothing more than a towel came back to her. She'd continually pushed it away, but it really wasn't an easy image to ignore.

Beyond irritated with herself and her weakness over a pretty face—and an even prettier physique—she forced herself to concentrate, ruthlessly pushing aside any stray thoughts that tried to sneak into her head. For the next several hours, she gave one hundred percent of herself to this risk assessment. And, thankfully, in the end she put together a great report. One that Frank seemed impressed with as he flipped through it while she waited to see if he wanted any revisions.

"Well done, Rachel. I know I can always count on you. I'll let you know if I have any questions after I dig in deeper."

Walking out of Frank's office, she breathed a sigh of relief just as her cell phone rang. It was Morgan calling.

"Hey, sis, sorry to bother you again," Morgan said in a rasping voice that made it clear she wasn't yet all better, "but would you mind doing me another favor by giving Nicholas a ride out to my studio in about thirty minutes? Grams dropped by with some chicken soup yesterday and told me how you went the extra mile to get him to her house. I owe you big-time for being so helpful."

Silently, Rachel wondered if Nicholas would agree that being picked up from the ferry a half hour late and then having a six-year-old get sick all over him in the backseat of a car could be considered *going the extra mile* and *being so helpful.* But of course all she said to her sister was that she would be more than happy to go pick him up again.

Yesterday, she had looked awful with axle grease all over her. So while she couldn't get a chance to make a new first impression, she decided she could certainly make a better second one. Not because she wanted anything to happen with Nicholas, of course. And not because anything was *ever* going to happen with him, even if she did want it. She simply couldn't stand the idea that he would remember her as someone who looked as if she'd just got off shift as a NASCAR mechanic.

Once home, Rachel changed into dark blue skinny jeans and a silky pink top that Morgan had brought her as a present from Fashion Week in New York City. Casual but stylish. She took her time fixing her lip gloss and eye shadow, too. Again, she told herself that it wasn't about impressing Nicholas. It was simply a question of taking pride in her appearance. Just because she was a single mother didn't mean she had to look ragged all the time, did it?

Rachel was just about to head out when her boss called. "Hi, Frank. I'm guessing you want to check on some figures?"

"I was taking a closer look at the data on diving accidents in relation to salvage and noticed that you hadn't broken them down by depth of water here, so—"

"Frank, can you hang on for a sec?" Rachel said, interrupting him mid-sentence when she heard someone knocking. "There's someone at the door."

Rachel was shocked to find Nicholas standing on her front step, holding a huge stuffed rabbit in one hand, looking every bit as handsome as he had after getting out of the shower. Although, unfortunately, wearing more clothes today.

Unfortunately? She meant *fortunately*!

"I was just coming to pick you up from Grams' house to take you over to Morgan's studio," she said, so stunned to see him that she forgot to even say hello first.

"It's a nice day," Nicholas offered by way of an explanation. "I thought I'd walk over and save you that part of the journey. I got this for Charlotte." He held up the toy rabbit. "I hope it will help make her feel a little better."

It was such a sweet gesture that Rachel felt her heart melt in her chest. Sexy *and* sweet was quite a combination...one she was finding harder to resist by the second.

"She's actually fine today," Rachel told him, smiling as she thought about how wonderfully resilient her little girl was. "She woke up and went to school as if nothing had happened yesterday. She's even at dance practice now. But it was so kind of you to think of her."

He smiled back, then pointed to her phone in her hand. "Is there someone on the line?"

Oh no! She'd forgotten all about her boss. Gesturing for Nicholas to come inside and put down the stuffed rabbit, she said, "Sorry about that Frank. You'll find breakdowns by water depth in Appendix C." After she answered a couple of other quick questions, she hung up, then told Nicholas, "Let me just get my keys, and we can head out."

"No rush. Everything will work out fine."

Rachel wished life could really be that easy, that she didn't always have to feel like she was needed in three places at once or everything would just fall apart.

When they got out to her car, she realized he was missing something. "No surfboard today?"

"People have seen me surfing plenty of times. With this show, I'll get to introduce the audience to a bunch of fun new sports, like rock-climbing, parasailing and hang gliding."

Dangerous new things, by the sound of it. But she wasn't here to try to talk Nicholas out of anything. She was just there to get him to her sister's studio. And if there *was* a part of her that thought those sports actually sounded like the most fun imaginable? Well, Rachel would just keep pointedly ignoring it. Just the way she'd been working so hard to ignore the memory of Nicholas wearing nothing but a towel...

"This really is a beautiful island," Nicholas said as Rachel drove.

"I agree," Rachel said, "but you must have seen plenty of beautiful places before now. I mean, you're from Hawaii, which sounds amazing."

"Hawaii is definitely amazing, but just because Walker Island isn't all white sand and tropical beaches doesn't mean it isn't incredible in its own right. At least, from what I've seen of it."

For a moment, Rachel was hit with the urge to offer to show him more of it. The berry fields with their surrounding wild flowers. The cliffs on the north side of the island. Even the small town had a kind of quaint antiquity to it that would be great to walk through with Nicholas beside her. She could easily imagine sitting with him on one of the small beaches.

But she knew she couldn't afford to think like that, couldn't let herself be drawn in even deeper by him. Not when he would be leaving the island just as soon as he'd finished having his adventures for the TV show. The last kind of man she needed in her life was one who didn't have a prayer of staying in one place.

"I had assumed you'd only be interested in the waves around the island."

"Good waves are definitely a bonus, but often the best parts of my job are the places I get to visit. Thailand, Australia, Brazil."

"And now Walker Island," Rachel said with a smile.

"Yes," he agreed with a smile. "Walker Island is definitely one of my new favorite places. And I have to say that staying with your grandmother is a lot of fun. She is such an interesting woman."

"What about Emily and Paige?" Rachel asked. "Did you get a chance to spend some time with them last night?"

She could imagine Paige—lithe and athletic from hours of dancing every day—being the kind of woman Nicholas would go for all too easily. If the two of them did connect, Rachel vowed not to be jealous. Paige was one of the sweetest people on the planet and deserved to be happy. If a fling with a gorgeous surfer would make Paige happy, Rachel would support her sister. No matter what.

"Actually, no, I haven't met them yet."

"Weren't they home for dinner last night?"

"I'm not sure. I was out, and by the time I got back, everyone was already asleep."

Rachel could easily imagine the kind of activities that might have kept Nicholas out that late. The island had plenty of opportunities for tourists who wanted to have a good time.

"You never told me what you do for a living," Nicholas said, breaking the sudden silence.

"Oh, you don't want to hear about that," Rachel insisted. "If I start talking about my work, you'll be bored in about five seconds flat."

"It isn't ever boring to hear a smart, sexy woman talk about something she's passionate about."

Rachel flushed slightly at the *smart, sexy* part of his reply. Was he flirting with her? She'd felt the spark between them when they'd met, and part of her wanted to believe that it might be possible to reach out and touch it, but she was too smart—and too wary—to let herself risk getting burned by another gorgeous man who flitted from port to port even faster than her ex had.

"How do you know that I'm passionate about my work?"

"Why would anybody spend their time doing something that they aren't passionate about?"

Most people lived lives where they had to do whatever was needed to meet their responsibilities. But it occurred to her that Nicholas had probably never even *had* a normal job, so it was no wonder that he could be so idealistic.

"I work as an actuary."

"That's fascinating."

"You're joking, right?"

He was clearly surprised by her response. "Why are you assuming I'd find that boring?"

"How can a guy in your line of work not find the idea of sitting in an office, assessing risks and looking at ways of managing them for insurance purposes at least a little bit boring? Especially when everything you do is such an adrenaline rush? And so incredibly dangerous, too." She was well on a roll now, but couldn't seem to stop herself from adding, "Did you know that in a recent study, 38.4% of a group of surfers had suffered an injury bad enough to keep them out of the water in the year just before the study was done?"

"That's the New South Wales report, isn't it?"

"You know the report?"

"Trust me, I know *exactly* how dangerous the sports I do can be, but just because surfing can be dangerous, it doesn't have to be. Not if you take the right precautions. When I'm teaching surfing, my students have to learn my safety routines before they get near a board." He grinned at her as he said, "Handing them my big laundry list of safety checks comes as a shock to some of them."

Not as much of a shock as it was to Rachel. Serious safety checks and insurance statistics simply didn't fit with his daredevil image. They did, however, serve to make him more alluring...especially on the heels of showing up with the surprise gift of a stuffed rabbit for her daughter.

Morgan was standing in front of her studio when they drove up. Her normally glowing sister still looked horribly drained and washed out— not even close to a hundred percent.

"Morgan, you should still be in bed." Rachel put an arm around her sister. "I'm going to take you back to your cottage now, and I'm not going to take no for an answer."

The three of them left the studio and headed across Morgan's property to her house. Once they were inside, Morgan said, "I'm so sorry I haven't been able to greet you better than this, Nicholas. Grams was so pleased to meet you, though."

"Your grandmother is great." He smiled at Rachel. "Your sister, too."

Morgan momentarily lit up at that comment, then turned to Rachel and said, "I know I've been asking for a lot of favors lately, but is there one more thing you could do for me?"

"Absolutely." Rachel would do anything for her sisters. "What do you need?" Hopefully, it would be something that took her far away from Nicholas and all of his sweet and sexy smiles that kept making her all melty inside.

"The film crew just informed me that they'd like to shoot an outdoor test segment with Nicholas today rather than starting in the studio. But as you can see, I'm just not up to it. Would you mind taking him down to where they've set up by the cove?"

Even if Rachel could have said no to her sister, she simply wasn't strong enough to turn down the chance for a few more minutes with Nicholas.

"No problem, Morgan. Just rest and get better, okay? And don't worry about a thing."

If only Rachel could do the same herself. But with her feelings for Nicholas growing deeper by

the second, she was suddenly more worried than
ever.

CHAPTER SEVEN

It was only a short walk from Morgan's house down to the sandy and sheltered cove, which was especially pretty with the wild flowers all in bloom around it. The breeze coming in off the water made it just a touch cooler than the rest of the island, but it was still warm enough to be pleasant and relaxing.

The film crew—a camera operator, a sound technician, and a production assistant—were already down on the sand with a tent full of gear, a small dinghy, and a kayak. "Looks like they've got everything we need to go kayaking," Nicholas said.

"We?" Rachel's eyebrows went up as she looked down at the kayak on the sand again and finally noticed that it was a two-person kayak. She shook her head. "No way."

"Come on, it will be fun," Nicholas said. "Everyone, this is Rachel Walker. She's going to be standing in for Morgan for our test shots while she's recuperating from her cold."

Before Rachel could explain that Nicholas was mistaken and that she would definitely *not* be getting into the double kayak with him, the woman behind the camera stepped away from it and looked her over with a nod. "You will be a perfect stand-in for Morgan, thanks so much for helping us out today." She turned back to Nicholas. "We should get going while the light is still perfect."

"But—"

The male sound technician cut Rachel off as he came forward with the mics. "I'll just need to get you both quickly rigged up."

"I don't think you understand," she tried again, "I only came down to the beach to—"

But the production assistant, a young woman in her twenties, was already leading Rachel toward the tent. "I'll just help you get into the wet suit, and then we'll be ready to go. It looks like you and Morgan must be close to the same size, aren't you?"

"Yes, we are," Rachel said automatically, before she stopped herself. "But since I'm not going out on the kayak, I don't want to waste any more of your time."

"Wait," Nicholas said. "Why aren't you going with me?" He looked genuinely puzzled by her protests. "You would enjoy it."

Yes, she would. She'd always loved kayaking in the ocean.

Rachel shook her head, forcefully clearing away that thought. That was the *old* her. She was older now, more mature. And a mother. Surely, she wouldn't enjoy the cold and wet and danger of being out on the ocean anymore.

"Why can't you just take the kayak out yourself?"

"The concept of my show isn't about me taking solo adventures and showing off my outdoors skills. It's meant to be about ordinary people having extraordinary adventures. The TV executives have seen me on screen by myself plenty of times before, but more than anything with these test shots they need to see how the two-person plan will work."

Rachel didn't know as much about how TV worked as Morgan or Hanna, but she knew enough to know that TV executives didn't like to guess about anything. They liked a sure bet. Which meant Nicholas really did need a partner for these test shots in the kayak today.

"Besides," he added, "I'd like to get out on the water with you. I think you'd enjoy it. Or am I wrong?"

Even though she was so incredibly tempted, Rachel made herself remind both of them, "I don't do adventure. I'm an actuary. One with a young daughter who depends on me. What would happen to Charlotte if something were to happen to me?"

But Rachel already knew the answer to that, all too well. After her own mother had died when she'd been a little older than Charlotte, their father expressed his grief by becoming so wrapped up in his work that Emily and Grams had pretty much finished raising the rest of them. And as a result of all the changes and the upset, Rachel had grown wilder and wilder with every year that passed, taking far more risks than other teenagers did. Until she'd finally ended up pregnant and dumped by the boy she'd wrongly assumed would stick by her through thick and thin.

Rachel couldn't stand the thought of something like that happening to Charlotte, of her little girl being so lost in grief that she couldn't keep from acting out.

"I would never want you to do anything that you feel is too risky," Nicholas said in a gentle voice, meant only for her ears. "So if you really don't want to do it, we'll pack up for the day and wait for Morgan to feel better. Whatever you decide, it will all work out."

He seemed so confident, so certain, as if it was obvious that everything would be fine even if they let the first day of filming slide. Yet, how could it be? Rachel knew what a film crew cost to hire and how much money they would lose by pushing back a day. Plus, if the crew told the executives that Nicholas had decided to blow off a whole day of shooting because Rachel didn't want to take part—and that he hadn't even been able to persuade her to give it a go—what would the TV execs think? Would they trust Nicholas with his own show? Or would they end up deciding that he clearly wasn't up to the task of working with ordinary people like her?

"Okay," she said at last, "I'll do it."

"Are you sure? Because I don't want you to feel pressured into doing anything that makes you feel at all unsafe."

He risked his own safety practically every day, but the very sweet concern in his voice was the final push she needed to reach for the wet suit. The smile he gave her as she got ready to go kayaking with him warmed her all over, head to toe.

A few minutes later, he passed her a life preserver and strapped one on himself. "Just in case we do end up in the water. There's a whistle and a GPS attached to it in the unlikely event we get swept away from the boat, and the film crew will be nearby the whole time to help us if there are any problems. We'll also stay close to shore so that we can come back in at any time."

Rachel was impressed—and reassured—by this safety-conscious side to Nicholas. After they made their final preparations, they waited for the filming boat to go out first before pushing the kayak out into the water together. He showed her how to use the best grip on her paddle, then pushed them out and climbed in to take his own seat just behind her. His paddling was strong, and when she began to paddle as well, she quickly fell into a rhythm with him.

"You're doing great," Nicholas said. "Now, I'd

like to practice some basic turning and stopping before we go any further. We'll also try a couple of shallow-water drills to practice climbing back in if one of us should fall out."

That took up the next half hour, but the time seemed to pass far more quickly than that. Nicholas was such a patient teacher, and to Rachel's surprise, he didn't seem to be in a hurry to push her into more advanced techniques until she was ready. She had assumed that he would want to get her out onto the open ocean to guide the kayak through the bigger waves. Yet, he simply seemed to be happy being in the shallower waters with her. And the truth was that once she'd gotten over her initial concerns, it *was* really nice to relax out on the water, moving in perfect harmony as they paddled around the little cove.

"They thought about using this area as one of the sites for the island docks," she told him.

"When was that?"

"Back in my great-grandfather's day. It's closer to the berry fields and there aren't any big rocks on the way in, but the berry pickers who were starting to move to the island liked the current spot better because it is closer to town. From there, it's a clear shot over to Seattle, so they could get there a little easier on their days off, and it wasn't as far to bring building materials when they were first setting up."

"I love hearing about the history of the island. Is berry picking still a big industry here?"

"Yes, although these days we also get a lot of artists and marine researchers during whale-migration season."

"Speaking of whales, how do you feel about heading out a little further to see if we can spot any?"

Rachel had done that so many times as a kid, heading out in a small boat looking for whales. She used to love it, whether it was on a friend's small sailing dinghy or in a rowboat. In fact, she'd spent so much time swimming in the ocean as a kid that people had joked that she must have webbed feet. She could remember plenty of other good times, too. Parties in the caves near the cliffs on the north side. Running and climbing and laughing with a wide circle of friends.

Of course, back then she had blindly followed—and trusted—her feelings. Which had ended up giving her the amazing gift of her daughter. But, at the same time, it had also been more than a little traumatic when she'd realized that she was going to be a single mother.

Rachel wouldn't give up Charlotte for anything, but there had been enough pain associated with losing Guy and knowing he didn't want to even see his own child to persuade her to be more careful in the future.

Much more careful.

"Actually, do you think you have all the shots you need?"

"Probably, for today anyway," Nicholas said, "but I thought you were enjoying this."

"I am, but I should get back instead of looking for whales today." While she'd been paddling with Nicholas, it had been easy to forget about the work she still had to do to make up for being out of the office, the grocery shopping that needed to be done, not to mention the bathroom door that really needed a fresh coat of paint before she went to pick Charlotte up from dance class. "I have a lot of things I need to take care of."

"No problem, we can head back now." Nicholas was already paddling back toward the beach. After they'd gotten out of the kayak and were carrying it up the shore, he said, "Maybe when you're done with everything you need to take care of, we could get dinner?"

It seemed like such a simple offer, so casual. And, honestly, who wouldn't love to have dinner with a guy who not only looked like him, but who had been so thoughtful time and time again? Yet, she knew better than to let herself be tempted by not only this offer of dinner, but by all the other adventures that she could already sense he would want to take her on simply because that was who he was at his core.

"I don't think that's a good idea."

The look he gave her as they set the kayak down was full of questions about why she continued to push him away when they clearly had such great chemistry. Questions she wasn't at all prepared to answer because she was afraid they would reveal far too much.

But instead of asking her any of those

questions, he simply said, "Soon, I hope, you *will* think it's a good idea."

Flustered by his clear message that he wasn't giving up on her, even if he was going to let her refusal of his dinner invitation go tonight, she tried not to let it show as she politely asked him, "Can I give you a ride back to my grandmother's house?"

"I need to chat with the crew for a bit, but thank you for coming out with me on the kayak today. It really helped." He put his hand over hers. "And I really appreciate you taking a risk on me."

Even though she found she didn't like to imagine anyone else having fun with him out on the ocean, she said, "Hopefully, Morgan will be back on her feet by the time your next segment comes around." It wasn't easy to pull her hand away from his, but she made herself do it. "Good-bye, Nicholas."

A few minutes later, when she got back to her car, the only reason Rachel didn't leave tire tracks behind as she set off for home was because driving off at a high speed wouldn't have been safe. Although right then, the truth was that nothing felt particularly safe anymore.

Particularly the way she was feeling about the surfer with the sweet and sexy smile...

CHAPTER EIGHT

"We'll just add one last touch with the bow in the front of your dress," Rachel said that evening as she tied the satin ribbon into place on Charlotte's pink party dress. "Gorgeous!"

"Why do we need to look so pretty, Mommy?"

"Tonight's a very special night. All your aunts are going to be there, and Michael, Brian and Joel, and so are Grandpa Tres and Great-Grandma Ava."

Every year, the whole family met up for a big fall dinner, usually not long after Rachel's father had returned from leading his educational tours through Europe and was back teaching at the high school. It was the one time you could guarantee that all of the Walkers would be in the same room at the same time, with Morgan coming in from New York when she had lived there and Hanna taking the ferry in from Seattle.

Tonight, Rachel had decided they would walk

to Grams' house as she wanted to have a glass or two of wine with her family and she wasn't going to risk driving afterward.

"Is Aunt Hanna's hair still pink?"

"I'm sure it's some bright color," Rachel said with a laugh. "In any case, we'll find out for sure soon."

"Can I have pink hair?"

Rachel smiled at her daughter's question, one she'd known was coming. "I think your hair looks very pretty as it is."

"Will Nicholas be there?"

He wasn't family, but Grams always loved to include her houseguests in whatever events were happening while they were on the island. Still, Rachel said, "I don't know," because she didn't want to get Charlotte's hopes up, especially when her daughter was clearly hoping that he would be at the party. But he'd been too busy partying to have dinner with her grandmother and sisters the previous night, hadn't he?

They stopped for a few minutes to watch a butterfly, and by the time they arrived at Grams', Paige was at the door waiting for them. For once, she wasn't wearing dance gear, although she was still dressed in the elegantly understated way she favored.

"Rachel, Charlotte, there you are. The others just arrived, as well."

Charlotte rushed forward to hug her aunt. Before she'd started school, Charlotte had spent quite a lot of her free time down at Grams' dance school, where Paige did a lot of the teaching. The two of them were very close.

Not wanting to give herself away by immediately asking if Nicholas was also there, Rachel said instead, "How is Dad doing with Joel?" Their father had been away in Europe when Joel and Hanna had fallen in love. He'd said he was happy about their relationship, but a feud between their families had gone on for a long time—generations even—and it was obvious to all of them that their father was still trying to get used to having a Peterson as a new member of the Walker family.

"They're getting on just fine, thankfully," Paige said. "And Emily's in the kitchen, like always. I would have tried to help, but when Michael did, she immediately shooed him out of the room. And Morgan is obviously drinking cough syrup like water just to be here."

"Poor thing," Rachel said as she took Charlotte through to the dining room, where everyone was sitting around the huge wooden table. This room was the heart of the home Rachel had grown up in, and it said a lot about the Walker household that, even with everyone gathered together, it didn't feel overcrowded.

It felt just right.

Rachel made her way around the table, hugging each of her sisters and then her father and grandmother. Hanna had switched the streak in her hair from pink to blue, and Charlotte reached up to touch it when Hanna knelt down to say hello.

"No, you can't have your hair blue either," Rachel said to forestall the obvious question.

Beside them, Morgan smiled. "Hanna makes more changes to her hair than I do."

"That's because I'm behind the camera, not in front of it, so I can afford to be a continuity nightmare."

When Charlotte began to reach up to hug Morgan, her sister said, "I'm sorry, sweetie, it's better if you don't. I'm afraid I'm still full of germs."

Taking her seat, Rachel was struggling with a mixture of both relief and disappointment that Nicholas wasn't there, when suddenly he breezed in—sending her heart rate immediately flying. Charlotte made a sound of joy and immediately launched herself into his arms.

"Are you feeling better?" he asked her little girl.

"Yes," she replied as she hugged him tight, "and I love my new stuffed rabbit."

With a ruffle of her hair, he put her back down just as Grams said, "I was beginning to wonder where you'd gotten to. We can't have you missing dinner with us again." Rachel was surprised by the way her grandmother was calling Nicholas out on partying rather than spending time with them the night before. Ava wasn't usually so confrontational. But then she added, "Did everything go all right with the production company?"

"It all looks like it's going to be fine," Nicholas replied. "I've always loved family dinners, even when it isn't my family, and I really am sorry that dealing with the issues that came up with filming meant I had to miss dinner yesterday and that I'm racing in today, as well."

Rachel felt a pang of guilt that she had jumped to conclusions yet again, simply because his job was professional thrill-seeking. He hadn't been partying, he'd been working.

"I thought we had filled out all of the necessary paperwork for the permits, but they keep finding new documents for me to look over," he continued. "Fortunately, nothing needed to be notarized today. Although it was worth taking care of those permits yesterday, because otherwise Rachel and I wouldn't have been able to go out kayaking this morning."

"You talked Rachel into going kayaking with you?" The disbelief was clearly audible in Hanna's voice.

"Sure did," Nicholas said with a smile that felt like it was meant only for Rachel. "We found the perfect little cove on the beach just below Morgan and Brian's cottage, and Rachel agreed to go out in the double kayak with me while we filmed the first test segment."

She dearly appreciated that he didn't tell anyone just how much effort it had taken to get her into the kayak, or how she'd abruptly ended the outing. Instead, he made it sound as if it had simply been a fun day out for the two of them.

The ambience at the fall dinner was very different from the way it had been in previous years. The meal itself was as wonderful as ever—Emily always did such a great job on the food—but there were many more people, for one thing, what with Brian, Joel, and Nicholas.

"Have you ever surfed in Europe?" Rachel's father asked Nicholas. "I've just come back from that part of the world, and it seems hard to believe there's much surfing there."

"More than you might think," Nicholas assured him and started to describe some of the better surfing spots along the Mediterranean and farther north along the coast of England. "And even when there isn't much surfing, there's always something really interesting to do."

As Tres encouraged Nicholas to tell them about a climb he'd done in New Zealand, Rachel's thoughts drifted back to the time they'd shared in the kayak, just the two of them moving perfectly together over the water. For that brief time, her worries had drifted away on the tide...and it had been truly wonderful.

When Emily got up to bring in dessert, Rachel was surprised that her sister asked her to help in the kitchen. Once they were away from the dining room, Emily asked, "Are you okay?"

"I'm fine." But even to her own ears, she didn't sound particularly *fine.*

"Are you really? You seem a little preoccupied tonight."

Before Rachel could stop herself, she blurted,

"It's Nicholas."

Emily looked more closely at her. "What about him?"

Rachel barely knew where to start. "The gorgeous way he looks. The way he's so much sweeter than I expected him to be. The fact that he got me to go kayaking with him, and then, when we got out on the water..."

"It felt good?" Emily guessed.

"So good. But it shouldn't have."

"I don't understand. Why shouldn't being out on the ocean with a handsome man feel good?"

"Because it's not safe! *He* isn't safe. Nothing about him is safe, from what he does for a living to how he looks at me. And yet, I still can't stop thinking about him! It's so bad that I couldn't concentrate at work today after we went kayaking, even though I shouldn't be thinking about a guy like him in that way."

"Ah, I think I understand now," Emily said softly. "*Guy* is exactly the problem, isn't he?"

Rachel swallowed. "I don't know what you're talking about."

"Yes, you do. You're worried that Nicholas is just like Guy. You look at him, and you keep wondering if you're falling for the same man who abandoned you and Charlotte just like"—she snapped her fingers—"*that.*"

Knowing there was no point in continuing to deny it, Rachel nodded. "It's hard not to compare the two of them. I mean, when I first saw Nicholas, he was leaning against his surfboard on the docks and people were fawning all over him, telling him how great he is."

Emily put an arm around her. "But don't you see? You, more than anyone, know how to spot a fake now. And if you can't stop thinking about Nicholas, then I can't help but think there's a reason for it. That beneath his good-looking, adventurous surface, there must be something strong pulling you two together. After all," her sister added, "you did just say how sweet he is."

"Speaking of sweet," Rachel said by way of changing the subject, "we should probably take dessert out now." But all the while, she couldn't help wondering if her sister was right—and if she should risk giving Nicholas a chance.

CHAPTER NINE

After dinner, while Rachel helped Emily with the dishes, her sister was kind enough not to ask any more pointed questions. Probably because she could clearly see that Rachel was still thinking things through. Was Emily right about Rachel judging Nicholas by an unfair comparison to *Guy*? And if she was, how much of herself—and her carefully guarded heart—would she have to risk to find out whether he was truly different from her ex?

By the time she'd put away the final dish and headed back into the family dining room, Charlotte was busy playing cards with Nicholas.

"Go fish!" Charlotte said.

Charlotte had always been a happy little girl and was rarely happier than when she was playing cards. A couple of months back, she'd engaged Grams in a game of rummy that had gone on for hours until Grams had finally declared she was too tired to keep up. But Nicholas didn't seem to mind. In fact, he seemed to be enjoying the game and wasn't in any sort of rush to end it. But since Charlotte had school in the morning and it was already close to her bedtime, Rachel knew that they ought to get home.

"It's time to finish up the game so that we can get you home to bed."

"But, Mommy, I'm not tired." She might have been more convincing if she hadn't yawned just then. "Can't we stay at Grams' house? Nicholas is."

"That's because he's just visiting Walker Island. His home is a long way away on another island called Hawaii," Rachel explained. "Did you thank him for the bunny he gave you earlier?"

"I did," she replied, but turned back to Nicholas and said, "I totally love it."

"I'm totally glad," Nicholas replied with a warm smile.

"Now say goodnight to everyone. We've still got to walk home."

Charlotte didn't look happy about the game ending, and she *really* didn't look happy about walking home on top of that. Maybe walking over here had been a mistake. After all, for a tired six-year-old, it was quite a long walk back. Rachel figured she would probably end up carrying her at least part of the way home.

But right then, Nicholas stood up and held out a hand to Charlotte. "How about if I give you a piggyback ride home?"

Charlotte was already clambering up onto

Nicholas' back as Rachel said, "That's really nice of you to offer to carry her home, but then you'll have to walk back afterward, and—"

"It's fine," Nicholas assured her. "I don't mind doing the walk in both directions."

"It's fine, Mommy," Charlotte said, echoing him.

But was it actually fine?

The last thing Rachel wanted to do was encourage her daughter to become attached to someone who was going to be gone in a week. But at the same time, she didn't want her to be afraid of meeting new people. Plus, hadn't he just shared a meal with them where he'd fit in amazingly well with her family? And, if she were being totally honest with herself, didn't the idea of a moonlit walk with Nicholas make her own heart beat just a little bit faster?

"Okay, thanks," Rachel said, then went to hug each of her family members goodnight. She couldn't help but laugh when Nicholas carried Charlotte around so that she could do the same. Once all the good-byes had been said, he made a run for the door with Charlotte clinging to him.

"Come on, let's see how fast we can go."

Rachel set off after them, half-worried that he was serious. What if he fell? What if Charlotte lost her grip? But once she got outside, it was clear that he had only been teasing and was ready for a slightly more sedate walk back.

As they set out, Rachel could see that after her initial burst of energy, Charlotte was actually quite sleepy. Which meant that if Nicholas hadn't been there, she would have either ended up carrying her daughter all the way back home, or trying to coax her into walking despite how tired she was. No question about it, having Nicholas accompany them home was definitely the better choice.

"Do you and your family do that regularly?" Nicholas asked.

She nodded, then realized he might not be able to clearly see her in the moonlight. "Usually, Hanna is busy with her studies and filmmaking, Morgan is often off-island for her TV commitments, and Dad tends to be busy with the school and his educational trips. But for our fall dinner, everyone rearranges their schedules to make sure they can be on the island for the night."

"It must be nice having everyone you love around you."

It was, and the family get-togethers were wonderful. But at the same time, her sisters' successes with both career and love could also sometimes feel like a reminder that Rachel was not only still on the island working in insurance, but that she hadn't found anyone who made her heart beat as fast as her rotten ex had. When she was younger, she'd assumed that once she was old enough, she'd go off into the world to explore all of its exciting nooks and crannies. But that wasn't the way it had worked out.

Well, she thought, aside from the part about her heart beating fast. Because Nicholas certainly kept sending it into overdrive, with nothing more than one of his gorgeous smiles...

Once they got to the house, Nicholas carried Charlotte inside. After silently checking with Rachel to make sure it was okay, he headed for her room and laid her down gently on her bed. He did it so softly and quietly that Charlotte barely murmured in her sleep, rolling over and reaching for the stuffed rabbit Nicholas had given her.

Deciding it wouldn't hurt Charlotte to sleep in a dress instead of her jammies for one night if it meant getting a few extra minutes of sleep after such a busy evening out, Rachel pressed a kiss to her daughter's cheek and said, "I love you." Then she crept out of the room after Nicholas, who had headed back into the living room.

Once they were alone, it would have been so easy to reach for him. But she knew if she did, that one touch would inevitably lead to more. He would pull her even closer to him, their lips would meet, and—

Rachel swallowed instinctively at the heady thought. That was the problem. It was *too* good of a thought. Too good to ever be real. To ever be safe with a man like Nicholas.

Still, when she looked up into his eyes, the heat in them had her wondering if he would be the one to bridge the gap between them and kiss her impulsively, the same way he seemed to do everything else in his life. A part of her wanted his kiss so, so badly. But at the same time, despite the instinctive pull she felt toward Nicholas—one so strong that it had been there from the very first moment she'd set eyes on him at the ferry—the days when she could just dive into something on instinct were long gone.

As if he could sense her conflicting thoughts, instead of grabbing her and kissing her, he simply said, "You've got a great kid there. She's so bright and enthusiastic. She's going to go out and conquer the world one day."

A surge of pride rose within Rachel. It was true that Charlotte was precocious. She wanted to know, and do, and try everything. Yet, just the thought of what all those things *out there* might be—off the island, where Rachel couldn't do anything to protect her—was enough to bring fear a beat later. Nicholas was talking as though it was good that one day her daughter would be going out into a big, scary world full of dangers. But, then, of course he would think like that—his life of adventuring had worked so well for him that he assumed it would work just as well for everyone else.

"I want her to explore, but I can't stand the thought of her ever getting hurt."

"You've raised a smart kid. She'll know how to make the right decisions when the time comes. It'll be okay," Nicholas assured her.

"Until you have kids, you can't know how scary the world can be."

"Maybe not," he conceded, "but I still know how important family is."

Every time he talked about family—about

how much he was enjoying getting to know hers and how lucky she was to have them all nearby— a part of her started to think that maybe falling into his arms wouldn't be the worst thing in the world.

But she knew better, didn't she? Knew better than to fall for a gorgeous wanderer just because he said all the right things.

"If I had kids," he continued, "I would love them so much. And I know I would try to protect them, but I would want to show them everything the world has to offer, too."

"That's easy to say when you're too busy gallivanting around the world to bother having kids," she said in a deliberately crisp voice, one that she hated hearing coming out of her own mouth even if it was necessary to try to push him—and the desperate longing he made her feel—away.

"That's not why I don't have any children, Rachel."

She knew better than to ask, but she still couldn't stop the words from falling from her lips. "Then why?"

"I don't have kids because I hadn't met the right woman to have them with."

Oh God, why did she so desperately want that *right woman* to be her? And why was she teetering so precariously on the verge of throwing herself at him for a kiss that neither of them would ever forget?

But, then, drawing on six years of strength—

strength she'd had to learn the moment Guy had left her pregnant and alone—she said, "Thank you for walking us home, but I should really be heading to bed now. And I'm sure you've got a big day ahead of you with the film crew, too."

For a moment, when he moved closer, she thought he was going to kiss her anyway and try to convince her that going to bed alone wasn't even close to the right choice. And, despite all of the warnings she had been giving herself, she inwardly rejoiced.

But, in the end, he simply brushed his lips against her cheek and said, "Good night," leaving her heart racing in anticipation of the true kiss that she wanted more than she'd ever wanted anything in her life.

CHAPTER TEN

The next morning after Rachel got Charlotte ready for school, she decided to tidy up the house before logging into her email to see what new projects Frank might have waiting for her to work on. But even though this was her normal daily schedule, things didn't feel quite right this morning. Almost as if she was missing something. Or *someone*. Because for the first time in three days, she wouldn't be picking Nicholas up or taking him somewhere. Instead, Morgan had insisted—despite all of their protests last night— that she was feeling well enough to shoot the climbing segment today.

How was it, Rachel found herself wondering, that after only a couple of days, Nicholas had already become a part of her daily routine? And just because she knew better than to think a man like him could ever truly become part of anyone's day-to-day schedule, it still didn't do anything to ease the nagging sense of disappointment that had settled inside her that Morgan, instead of her, would be spending the day at the cliffs with him.

Thankfully, there was always something to do in a house with a messy six-year-old around— namely a thorough cleanup of Charlotte's room— so Rachel did her best to push that longing aside as she tidied up.

She didn't treat chores as a kind of meditation the way her sister Emily seemed to, but there was still something almost soothing about going through Charlotte's room, tidying away the clothes and the toys that lay scattered around. At least until her eyes settled on the new stuffed rabbit...and the shark tooth necklace it was now wearing.

Rachel could barely believe it—Charlotte had obviously taken Nicholas' necklace last night when he carried her home. And now, she knew she needed to return it to him immediately. Which meant driving over to the film location at the cliffs after all.

She knew all the good climbing spots on the island, so she was pretty certain she knew which spot Morgan would have chosen for today. Memories of her climbing days flashed through her mind—times spent scrambling up rock faces, often without safety ropes. She'd also climbed trees, buildings, anything that offered a challenge or a good view at the top.

How could she have been so reckless? What if she had fallen?

But I never did, did I?

* * *

By the time Rachel arrived at the base of the cliffs, though the production crew was clearly ready to film a climb, Nicholas and Morgan weren't anywhere near to starting. And as Rachel got closer, it was easy to hear their conversation.

"No, absolutely not. I'm sorry, Morgan, but there is no way you are climbing today." Nicholas looked very serious as he said it, reminding Rachel of the way he'd gone through the safety routines for their kayak trip. Clearly, he wasn't going to compromise on safety, not for a TV show or any other reason.

"Come on, Nicholas," her sister argued, "you've said yourself that you need normal people to go on your adventures with you. If we don't get the shots, then what's the point of coming here to film today?"

The film crew looked eager to get Morgan ready, but as the production assistant reached out to help her with her climbing harness, Nicholas stepped between them and shook his head.

"I'm not going to let you do it. I know you're only trying to help, but you simply aren't well enough yet." When it seemed Morgan wasn't going to listen, he added, "And what would the producers of your show think if I got their big star injured?"

Rachel saw Morgan try to laugh that off, but

the laughter turned into a coughing fit. "I'm not that big a star. Besides..."

Nicholas handed Morgan a bottle of water. "You are a big star as far as Brian and your family and friends who love you are concerned. And I don't think any of them would forgive me if I let you climb when you're feeling like this. I sure wouldn't forgive myself."

"You need to listen to him, Morgan," Rachel said as she finally came forward. "It was only a day or so ago that you were ready to fall over. Besides, it's not like you ever liked climbing anyway."

"But if I don't climb with Nicholas today," Morgan said, "who will?"

"I'll do it." The words were out of Rachel's mouth before she'd realized they were coming.

Had she really just offered to take Morgan's place again? Why would she do something as stupid as that?

Then again, she knew these cliffs and could still remember climbing this particular route a dozen times or more. Usually without many safety precautions. She shuddered, thinking of the risks she'd taken. But there was another part of her that was already looking up at the cliff face, planning the best route as if a piece of her past was calling to her. Again.

The production team was clearly eager for her to take over for her sister. "Actually, if you were to climb today, Rachel, we'd have really good continuity. Not to mention the fact that the two of you have great on-screen chemistry."

Well, she supposed there was no backing out now as a smiling Nicholas brought the climbing harness over and she stepped into it with the familiarity that experience brings.

"I've seen pictures of you climbing. Did you ever do it here?"

Though his mouth was so close to hers as he adjusted the straps that it was hard to think about anything other than kissing him—even the climb ahead—Rachel nodded. "Not for a long time, though."

"I'm sure you'll be even more of a natural on the cliffs than you were out on the ocean in the kayak," he told her. "Now, before we begin, we need to go through the safety words for climbing."

Behind him, the camera was rolling, yet this didn't feel anything like a rehearsed video presentation—it just felt real and natural. For many other people, this focus on safety would have felt like a waste of time, a task they undertook simply because they had to. Yet, with Nicholas, it felt as if he was genuinely giving her a climbing lesson, and all his attention was on her. Of course, though his attention had been on her for days, it hadn't been until this morning that she'd realized how much she had been missing it...or just how much she appreciated it.

"Don't start climbing until I say 'climb on,' and when you're ready to start, shout 'climbing' up to me. Rock faces can do strange things to sound."

"I remember."

He went through the other basic climbing communication words with her, covering everything from the essential "on belay" and "off belay" for managing the safety ropes, to the more urgent terms like "watch me" and "falling!"

"Although, hopefully," he added with a reassuring grin, "we won't need that last one."

For a moment, Rachel's actuary-trained brain couldn't help but think about the statistics for rock-climbing injuries and fatalities. It should have been all she needed as a reminder to herself that she shouldn't be doing this. That she couldn't be a wild, adventurous person anymore when she knew everything that could go wrong on climbs like this, from unsafe ropes to being struck by falling rocks.

And yet, here she was, taking the helmet Nicholas held out for her to wear. Both of their helmets had small video cameras on them. From there, it was a matter of focusing on the basics of hand- and footholds, the need to open her hips to stay close to the wall, and the importance of climbing with her whole body.

They were just getting ready to go when Rachel suddenly remembered the whole reason she had come to the cliffs in the first place. She reached into her pocket and pulled out the shark tooth necklace. "Charlotte took it," she said with an apologetic shake of her head. "I don't know why she did it, and I'll make sure she apologizes to you properly later, but I thought you'd want it back."

"Thanks, although she can have it if she wants it."

"She can?"

"The first surfer I ever met gave it to me. Am I the first surfer she's met?"

"You are."

"Then she should definitely have it. I'll just put it back on until I see her again."

"Aren't you angry that she took it?"

"Of course not. I know what it's like to not want to let something beautiful go." The way he said it made Rachel think he wasn't talking about the necklace anymore, but about *her.* "Plus, she's a good kid. That's all that matters. Are you ready to climb?"

To her surprise, she was. After she nodded, he turned back to the film crew, who gave them the thumbs-up.

"I'm climbing," Nicholas said, and set off up the rock face. Rachel watched as he locked in spikes and clamps, getting set to belay the first stage of the climb for her. "On belay," he yelled back down to her. "Climb on."

It was her turn now. Despite his instruction and her fairly clear memories of this route, the first few moves were still difficult. It was like her brain was trying to reject what her body already knew how to do, almost as if she'd lost her trust in her ability to climb.

But even though their climb started out slow,

Nicholas was there above her, waiting patiently. He kept just the right amount of slack on the rope as he belayed for her, giving her enough tension to feel supported without it turning into a restriction.

"You're doing really well," he called down. "Keep going."

At last, Rachel made it to the spot where Nicholas was waiting, wedged in on a small outcropping of rock. She was out of breath, and her limbs were a little shaky, but at the same time she felt incredibly—and wonderfully—alive.

"Now you belay for me while I do the next part. All right?" When she nodded, he said, "Climbing."

He headed up the rock face with easy, controlled movements, and she couldn't help but enjoy watching his well-honed muscles flex every time he stretched for a new handhold or foothold. She focused on keeping the right tension on the line as he climbed, knowing how much trust he was placing in her. If he fell, she was effectively all that stood between him and a long drop.

Fortunately, he made it to the top easily, disappearing up over the edge of the cliff. Which meant that it was her turn now, as he shouted down for her to climb on.

Slowly, she felt the rhythm of climbing these cliffs come back to her. How her body was meant to move, finding handholds with greater and greater certainty while her feet found purchase on familiar parts of the rock. As the old grips came back to her more quickly now, the world narrowed down to just her, Nicholas, and the craggy rock face.

And then, suddenly, her hand slipped as it reached for a hold that just wasn't quite there...

"Falling!"

Rachel went into free fall, the sky blue and big above her before the rope attached to her went tight, the harness digging into her as it took her weight.

But, actually, it was Nicholas taking her weight. And as she swung out from the rock face, she knew that she was completely in his hands. Because if he let go...

No, he wouldn't. Even breathing hard with her heart hammering in her chest, Rachel knew that he would *never* let go.

"I've got you," he called down. "I can lower you down to ground level easily if that's what you like."

Perhaps she should have said yes and let him slowly lower her to the ground, but she couldn't. Not here. Not now.

"I want to finish this. Help me get back to the wall."

Nicholas gently swung her back to the wall, and Rachel scrabbled at it. As soon as her hands and feet locked on, she yelled, "Okay, climbing!" She could still feel the adrenaline pounding in her, and it felt good. Really good. She concentrated on each handhold, determined that she wasn't going to let this beat her.

It was hard going. She'd lost ground when she fell and making that up meant more effort, more work for muscles that were already burning. She pushed on, though, and move by painstaking move she made her way farther up.

"You're doing really great," Nicholas called above her.

She began to move faster and faster as her instincts for climbing flooded back through her. Plus, it was so much easier to have confidence when Nicholas had already caught her and she knew for sure that he'd be there for her, no matter what.

"You're almost there," he called down to her, and she was amazed to look up and realize that in just a few more feet, she would be up over the lip of the cliff. Seeing the last few moves in her head, she completed them one after another, letting her feel for the climb guide her.

When Rachel finally pulled herself up over the edge, she rolled onto her back on solid ground once again, then looked over at Nicholas. If her legs hadn't felt so much like wobbly rubber at that moment, she knew she would have jumped up and kissed him.

In lieu of that, she smiled and said, "I did it."

"Yes," he said, his answering smile telling her just how proud he was of her achievement. "Yes, you did."

CHAPTER ELEVEN

At the top of the cliffs, Nicholas felt his own heart beat faster as he saw how ecstatically, joyously alive Rachel looked, despite the fall she'd taken halfway through the climb.

"Everything looks so beautiful from up here, doesn't it?"

"It does," he agreed, "especially when you get up here the hard way."

But the view wasn't anywhere near as beautiful as Rachel. He was so proud of her. She'd been so determined. Anyone else who hadn't climbed in years would have let him lower them down to ground level after the fall. But not Rachel.

Even more incredible was how she managed to combine her strength of spirit with being a mother. She'd done so well bringing up her little girl, creating such a safe, loving family for Charlotte.

"Are you ready to abseil back down now?" Nicholas asked.

"Yes, I think I've gotten my breath back enough now to head back to the bottom."

Most people he worked with didn't pay the kind of attention she did while he ran through the basic techniques for getting back down the cliff wall. And the look on Rachel's face as she stepped backward and deliberately pushed off into the air was so beautiful that he knew he would have lost control and kissed her just then if only he'd been able to fly through the air beside her.

The route down didn't take anywhere near as long as climbing up, and Rachel skipped easily from push-off point to push-off point. She was smiling broadly as they reached the bottom, not seeming to care at all that the cameras were on her, her happiness so big that he swore he could almost feel it inside of himself, too.

"That was great," Rachel said while Nicholas unclipped her. "Really, really great." She was practically bouncing in place.

He hoped she would want to celebrate her great achievement of climbing up the cliffs, because he was still on top of his own adrenaline rush. One that had far less to do with the climbing than it had to do with being near Rachel.

"We got some truly amazing shots!" Morgan said from her spot by the camera. "Although when you came away from the wall and started falling, Rachel, I almost had a heart attack."

"I was always safe," Rachel assured her.

"Nicholas had me."

That was true, but it felt great to hear her say it...and to also hear a brand new note of trust in her voice.

"Even so, you gave me a fright," Morgan said as she gave her sister a hug. "Come on, let's head back to my place and celebrate another good shoot. With copious quantities of cough medicine, in my case."

Nicholas smiled, because he'd been close to suggesting the same thing. But his smile faded a little when Rachel glanced at her watch and said, "I'd love to, but I have to go pick up Charlotte."

"In that case, maybe you can give me a ride back, too?" Nicholas suggested. He didn't want his time with her to end yet, and he knew his film crew would be busy working on edits for the rest of the afternoon.

After the way she'd pulled back after their kayaking trip, he had been expecting some hint of reluctance. This time, however, she smiled and said, "Sure, if you don't mind coming with me to pick up Charlotte first?"

"I'd love it." Climbing and surfing didn't frighten him, but the thought that he might have waited too long to have people like Rachel and Charlotte in his life...*that* was what was scary.

"In that case," Morgan said, "it looks like I'll just head home alone and tuck myself back in for a nap." She was clearly relieved to be able to go get some more rest.

After dropping Morgan off, as the two of them

headed toward Charlotte's school in Rachel's car, Nicholas thought about asking her to be his volunteer for all the other pieces they still needed to shoot around the island. After doing both the kayaking and climbing segments with her, he knew for sure now that she would enjoy it. But at the same time he had a pretty good sense that trying to push her into anything would only make her push back even harder.

Things had always worked out for him before, though. Surely, things with Rachel would, too, wouldn't they? After all, hadn't she found her way into this shoot today, even when it had been Morgan who was supposed to have been taking part? He was more thankful than ever that Charlotte had "borrowed" his shark tooth. If not for that, Rachel wouldn't have come to the cliffs.

Charlotte was waiting outside when they got to the school, and Nicholas loved watching the two of them hug, both of their mouths wide with radiant smiles.

"Nicholas," Charlotte exclaimed, "you're here again!"

"I am and happy to see you, as always."

But after she glanced at the shark tooth that was back around his neck, she didn't quite meet his eyes. "Are you sure you're happy to see me?"

"Of course I am."

Rachel leaned down and whispered something to her daughter. Charlotte's face was flushed as the brave little girl made herself look him in the eye. "I'm sorry. I shouldn't have taken your necklace."

"It's all right," Nicholas assured her with a smile. "In fact, I was hoping you would accept it as a gift."

Charlotte's eyes grew as big as saucers. "You want to *give* it to me?"

"The first surfer I ever met gave it to me. And since I'm the first surfer you have ever met, I think you should have it now."

With great ceremony that he could see positively thrilled the six-year-old, he drew the necklace off of his own neck and placed it around Charlotte's.

"Mommy, look! Nicholas gave me his necklace!"

"And it looks amazing on you, sweetie. Just remember, you'll have to take it off every night before you go to bed so that it doesn't poke you while you're sleeping."

"Okay," Charlotte said as she ran her fingers gently over the smooth, cool shark tooth and the rougher leather that held it in place around her neck, "I'll remember. I promise. My rabbit can wear it when I'm sleeping."

Rachel put an arm around her daughter and gave her a gentle squeeze. "How about if we go to the playground and get ice cream?"

Charlotte jumped up and down. "Ice cream!"

"Ice cream sounds good to me, too," Nicholas agreed.

They headed over to a local playground where a couple of moms sat on the benches while their kids played in the sandbox or clambered over a large climbing frame. From the nearby ice cream store, Charlotte chose strawberry, Nicholas had mint chocolate chip, but Rachel was the truly wild one in the bunch when she ordered a double cone with mint and mango. At his surprised look, she laughed and said, "It's an acquired taste. Want some?"

Even though he'd risked plenty around the world over the years, the only reason he dared to risk that particular taste combination was because of all the risks she'd already taken with him. Surely, he could take one for her now. And in the end, he was pleasantly surprised by how good the unexpected combination tasted.

As they walked around the edge of the playground, Nicholas' phone started dinging with photos the production team was sending him from the climb today. In all of them, Rachel was clinging to the rock face, looking determined and fearless and *happy*.

"Rachel, Charlotte, look at these photos they just sent from the shoot today." He held out the phone to them. "Aren't they great?"

"That's *you* climbing a rock, Mommy?"

"Yes, that's me."

Charlotte's eyes were wide as she looked from the phone to her mother. "You look like a superhero."

Rachel's smile broadened. "You know what? For a while there, I felt like one, too."

Charlotte quickly finished her ice cream then

ran off to play, leaving Rachel and Nicholas sitting together on the bench. To an outsider, Nicholas figured they must look like a couple who had come to the playground together with their daughter.

He liked that idea...quite a lot, actually.

If she had been any other woman, Nicholas would have kissed her days ago. He would have gone with the flow of his feelings and seen where it led. But with Rachel, he'd held back because he wanted to be certain. And he also wanted to make sure that he didn't scare her off. Yet, sitting here with her now in the sunlight after a great afternoon together, everything felt just right.

"Rachel."

Nicholas moved a little bit closer, and when she looked at him, he could see anticipation in her eyes. At the same time, though, he thought he also saw a small spark of fear. But that same initial fear on the cliff face hadn't stopped her from getting all the way to the top, had it?

"Mommy, look! I can climb just like you!"

Rachel abruptly pulled back from him to look over at Charlotte, who was clinging to the bars of the climbing frame, swinging a few rungs off the ground. She wasn't very high yet, but she was doing a passable—and very cute—imitation of her mother's earlier climbing exploits.

"Charlotte? What are you doing all the way up there? You've never been that high before."

"I'm climbing just like you did!" As if to emphasize her point, Charlotte moved up another rung.

"Be careful!" Rachel called out as she got up to rush over. And when Nicholas saw Charlotte's foot start to slip slightly and her grip loosen, he moved as quickly as he ever had to lift her off the bars and put her gently down on the ground.

"Maybe you'd better stay a little lower for a while," Nicholas suggested. "At least until you're bigger."

"I am big," Charlotte insisted. "I'm nearly six and a half!"

"Not too big to play in the sandbox, surely?" Rachel asked.

In lieu of answering, Charlotte immediately ran off to play in the sand. As Rachel stared after her daughter, she looked a little bleak. "Maybe I shouldn't have panicked just now, but she's just so important to me..."

"You and Charlotte are amazing together." He didn't want to make the mistake of pushing her too far, too fast, but he had to ask, "What happened, Rachel? Where is her father?"

Rachel led the way back to the bench, and they sat together in silence for a few moments, before she finally said, "Plenty happened with her father, back when I was younger. He was the only boy back then who could keep up with me when I wanted to go out climbing, or skiing, or any other wild thing I could think of."

"What changed?"

"Guy was fun, but he was irresponsible. He didn't see that at some point, you have to take life seriously. The moment things got serious when I found out I was pregnant...he left."

"Then he was a selfish idiot and not worth either one of you."

"I know that." Rachel touched her fingertips to her lips then, and he knew she was thinking of the kiss that had almost just happened right here on the park bench. "You're a good-looking, successful guy in his thirties. Most men like you would be married with kids by now, but you've never wanted that, have you?"

He wouldn't lie to her, even if it might make the going easier right now. "I've always taken life as it comes. I never had a firm plan, because I had never met the right person." *Until now.*

"How are you ever going to meet the right person if you keep running from place to place?"

"I'm not your ex," he replied in a gentle voice.

"I know you're not, because Guy was just a kid. We both were. You're different. I've seen that again and again since you and I met at the ferry. And yet..."

"I'm doing what I love, Rachel. And I know you understand, because I saw your face on the cliff today, saw how full of joy you were as you made your way to the top with me." He reached out to cup her cheek, partly because he couldn't resist touching her, but also because he wanted her to look him in the eye. "The way I see it, doing what I love means that any woman I meet sees the real me. And I've always known that the woman I finally fall in love with will be one I can share those beautiful moments with." He wanted so badly to kiss her, but knew reaching her this way first was so much more important. "The view from the cliff was beautiful, wasn't it, Rachel?"

Her eyes were the deepest, most beautiful blue he'd ever seen as she held his gaze. "Yes, it was. So beautiful it took my breath away."

His heart had never felt so full before. Or so thankful. Especially when she added, "Thank you for catching Charlotte. And thank you for catching me, too."

He moved his hand from her cheek to take hers in his. "Anytime."

CHAPTER TWELVE

"Look, Mommy! I made a picture."

Rachel turned from the stove to look at the picture her daughter was holding up of two figures on something brown and slightly jagged. "Is that Nicholas and me climbing?"

Charlotte frowned as though it ought to be obvious. "Yes! And I'm going to put it on the fridge so that you can remember what you did today." The fridge was their own little art gallery with pictures held in place by magnets. After Charlotte took the picture and pinned it in place with a frog-shaped magnet, she asked, "When will I be big enough to go climbing?"

"Not for a long, long time, sweetie. Climbing is dangerous."

"But you did it."

"I did," she agreed, "but Nicholas had to help keep me from falling."

"I like him, Mommy. Do you like him, too?"

"Of course I do," Rachel replied, but she could tell that it was clearly time to change the subject from Nicholas, and fast, before Charlotte's questions got any more probing. "In a few years when you're old enough, I'll see about taking you climbing with all the safety equipment. But for now, why don't you help me make dinner? I know you always like it when Aunt Emily lets you help her cook."

Rachel couldn't help but think about Nicholas as she helped Charlotte shape dough for the rolls they would be having tonight with dinner. She supposed it was inevitable that he'd be in her thoughts after the day they'd had together...especially after how close they'd come to kissing at the playground.

She had been so tempted to close that final inch between them. She could easily imagine what their kiss would have been like. Good. *Better* than good. Probably the best kiss of her life. In fact, it was impossible to imagine a guy like Nicholas kissing any way but perfectly. And after that...

No, stop that, Rachel! Thinking about Nicholas and his kisses was extremely dangerous—far more than even climbing the cliffs had been.

"Mommy, will he be coming for dinner tonight?"

Rachel started at that, almost dropping the saucepan she had just picked up. "No, sweetie. I don't think so. Why would he?"

"He came to dinner at Grandma's house."

"That's because he's staying at Grandma's house," Rachel explained. "There's lots of room for him there."

"There's lots of room here." Charlotte began to gesture with the spoon she was holding, and Rachel quickly lifted her down off the stool before she could knock over any of the hot pans.

"Careful, sweet girl."

"Okay, Mommy." It was what she always said when Rachel told her to be careful, but that didn't stop her from worrying that Charlotte might burn herself, or fall and break a bone...or grow up to fall in love with a man who wasn't safe.

Rachel forced herself to push that thought aside as she went back to preparing their dinner—meatballs with fresh-baked rolls, one of Charlotte's favorites. A short while later, when Rachel put a plate in front of her daughter at their small, round dining table, she tried not to think about just how nice it would have been if Nicholas were actually there with them for dinner. Knowing him, he'd likely entertain both of them with stories of all the adventures he'd had in far-flung corners of the world that Rachel had always meant to visit.

When they were finished eating and Rachel had done the dishes, she got out her computer while Charlotte played in the living room. The new report Frank wanted put together wasn't anywhere near as complex a job as the report for the salvage company, just a quick assessment of the risks for the owner of a small boat who planned to take tourists on whale-watching trips. But though she had put together reports for similar ventures dozens of times, after fifteen minutes of having to look up statistics multiple times, Rachel asked herself, "Why is this so hard?"

"What's hard, Mommy?" Charlotte looked up from playing with her new stuffed rabbit.

"Just something I'm trying to take care of for work." And she was still trying another fifteen minutes later, because she simply couldn't focus tonight. Not when what should have been an easy job felt like an intrusion on a day that had included so much happiness and excitement.

She was looking up the figures for the umpteenth time when she suddenly heard a loud clatter. She'd jumped halfway out of her seat by the time she realized that Charlotte had gotten into the closet where Rachel kept the ironing board and had pulled it out.

"Charlotte!" Rachel rushed over to her. "Are you okay?"

"It's heavy, but it didn't fall on me," Charlotte told her. "I wanted to play surfing, like Nicholas does."

Nicholas again. Rachel struggled to keep her composure. Trying to copy him could have gotten Charlotte hurt. "I know they have the same shape, but surfboards and ironing boards aren't the same thing at all. Now, how about if we put it back and then you can pick out a story for the two of us to read?"

Her daughter reluctantly nodded, but fortunately she loved reading stories together, so she was soon enraptured by the story she'd picked out of her bedroom bookcase. Charlotte often ended up making up her own stories long before they got to the end of whatever book they were reading, which Rachel normally loved. But tonight, she was worried about how everything seemed to be circling back to Nicholas when what had started off as a simple fairy tale quickly turned into a story about a wall-climbing, surfboard-riding princess who wore a dragon-tooth necklace that had magic powers.

Gently directing Charlotte's attention back to the story, Rachel got them back on track for a while, until her little girl abruptly asked, "When is Nicholas coming back to our house again?"

"I'm not sure," Rachel replied, even though she had been wondering the same thing herself. "He's very busy right now filming a TV show like your Aunt Morgan does." With that, she kissed Charlotte on the forehead and said, "It's getting late. Let's get you ready for bed."

A short while later, Charlotte was in her jammies, her teeth were brushed, and she was just getting ready to turn out the light when she asked, "Mommy, will we see Nicholas tomorrow? He's nice, and I really want to see him."

Rachel knew how attached her daughter could get to people she cared about. Just look at the way she'd followed Morgan around when she'd first come back to the island. The way she still followed Morgan around, come to think of it. Charlotte made attachments quickly, and those attachments stuck.

"He is very nice," Rachel agreed, "and it's good that you like him, but he's just a friend of Morgan's. He can't stay here on Walker Island with the rest of us."

"Why not?"

"Because he has other places he needs to be and things he needs to do. He was never planning to stay."

"But Aunt Morgan wasn't going to stay and she did."

Rachel reached down to stroke Charlotte's hair. "Your aunt is a special case."

"Can't Nicholas be a special case, too?"

I wish. "I'm sorry, sweetie. Things don't always work out like that."

"But that's not fair."

And as Rachel gathered her daughter into her arms and rocked her until she fell asleep clutching the stuffed rabbit to her chest, she also found herself wishing that Nicholas could stay.

CHAPTER THIRTEEN

The next morning, Rachel woke up more determined than ever. As soon as Charlotte went to school with her aunt and grandfather, Rachel walked over to her grandmother's house. She wanted to get there before Nicholas would have a chance to get caught up in hang gliding or skydiving—or whatever adventure was planned for today's filming.

But it was better not to think about his adventures, because from there it was only a small step to imagining herself doing them alongside him. She could all too easily imagine him running through the safety protocols for jumping out of a plane or shouting encouragements as he rode beside her on an extreme bike trail.

Only, there was no way of guaranteeing that he would *stay* beside her. Which was why she had to take care of the situation now, before things got any more complicated.

When she arrived at Grams' house, Nicholas was out in the garden, enjoying the plants and the views. His face lit up when he saw her. "It was already a beautiful day, but now that you're here, it's a stunning one."

From any other man it would have sounded like a practiced line, but for all her wariness, she couldn't shake the sense that Nicholas truly meant it.

"I'm sorry to bother you so early." Rachel felt more than a little nervous now that they were face-to-face again. "I know you're probably just about to leave to meet with the crew."

"Given the way you saved the last two shoots, I don't think anyone is going to complain about you showing up to chat with me for a few minutes this morning. Especially when seeing you always puts a smile on my face."

But Rachel wasn't so sure that his smile would remain. Not after she made herself tell him what she knew she needed to say. Or maybe he *would* just smile and then move on to the next thing by telling himself that "it would all work out" the same way he seemed to handle everything else in his life.

She took a deep breath before saying, "The last few days have been great. I've enjoyed them a lot, and so has Charlotte."

"The two of you deserve to enjoy every day, Rachel. What you have is so special."

She shook her head. "Please, Nicholas. This

isn't easy for me, and when you say such sweet things, it only makes it harder. You see, Charlotte's getting confused. She's been asking about you, wondering where you are all the time."

"I know exactly how she feels. I want to see more of her—and you—too," Nicholas said. "Why is that a problem?"

"Because she's gotten it into her head that you and I are involved."

"I'd like to be," he said softly. "And when you're not trying so hard to fight it, I'm pretty sure you would, too."

Feeling as though he could see right through her, she blurted, "Everything we've done together the past few days has been fun, but we both know that any connection you and I have is just one big accident. I was simply doing some favors for my sister, and they spiraled out of control."

"Sometimes," Nicholas said as he moved closer, "being out of control can be a good thing."

Once upon a time, that was exactly what she'd thought. But she'd learned better by now, which was why she told him, "Only if there's a safety net there to catch you when things go wrong."

"I will always be there to catch you if you'll let me."

Rachel flashed back to the moment when she'd been hanging from the cliff and how he'd kept her perfectly safe by holding her steady from up above. And then, afterward, how close—how very close—they'd come to kissing at the playground.

Knowing she couldn't afford to let him touch her, because she wouldn't be able to maintain her resolve if he did, she made herself take a step back from him rather than closer, the way she so desperately wanted to. One touch would easily be enough to have her begging for more.

She swallowed hard before making herself finish saying what she'd come to say. "I'm not suggesting that we should completely avoid one another while you're still here on the island. I just need us to keep things simpler and easier for Charlotte to understand. Because it isn't fair to confuse her by letting her think that we're more than we are. I need to be able to be honest with her about what's happening."

"If you really want to be honest," he said in a voice that was far more serious than any she'd heard yet from him, "then you need to admit how much I already mean to you. And you also need to understand how much you already mean to me."

"Just because we've had fun together on the island doesn't mean we're right for one another. You take risks for a living, while I make a living out of avoiding risks!"

Nicholas finally closed the rest of the distance between them and took her hands in his. "Has it ever occurred to you that the reason your daughter thinks there's something between us is because kids see what's really there?"

Rachel shook her head. "No, you're wrong. There can't be anything between us."

"Yes, there can," Nicholas insisted, his hand moving up to touch her hair. "Because there already is."

He didn't pause this time, didn't wait for her to be ready for him to make a move as he leaned in and kissed her with more passion than Rachel had ever imagined. His lips met hers like a wave meeting the beach, and like a wave would, the sensation washed over her.

She kissed him back on instinct, unable to stop herself, just the way she'd been unable to keep herself from wanting to climb the cliffs. She thought she could taste the sea on Nicholas' lips as she kissed him—and it thrilled her that she could taste the danger and adventure in him, too. She held tightly to him as she kissed him breathlessly, wanting—and needing—so much more than she ever had before.

She'd marshaled her thoughts so carefully before coming to see him this morning. She'd worked out exactly what she would say. But she had never expected anything like this, for all of her carefully considered reasons to fade away like the mist, torn apart by the pure, sweet sensation of a kiss. All she could feel was hands tangled in her hair, the rapid-fire pace of her heart beating in her chest...and a desire so intense it stunned her.

When they finally pulled apart, Rachel's head was buzzing with even more than the adrenaline rush she'd felt at the top of the cliff. There was nothing safe about kissing Nicholas. And certainly nothing sensible about it.

Yet now that they'd kissed, she felt more alive than she ever had before.

"Rachel?" Nicholas reached out to touch her cheek, and for a moment, just a moment, she thought he might be about to kiss her again. Instead, he softly said, "All the risk assessments in the world can't tell us anything about our connection right now. And they can't tell what's in our hearts, which is all that really matters. Don't you think it's okay to take a risk now and then, especially if that risk has a chance to make you truly happy?"

And the truth was that with his kiss still tingling on her lips, it was almost possible to believe that what they felt, what they wanted, counted for more than the rest of the world with all its disasters and dangers.

"Come back and do another segment with me tomorrow."

Nearly as tempted by that as she'd been by his kiss, instead of outright saying no the way she knew she should, she said, "Haven't they found anyone else they can talk into doing death-defying stunts alongside you?"

"There isn't anyone who has the same chemistry with me."

"You could work with anyone and make them look good."

"Not as good as you look," Nicholas assured her.

Rachel couldn't keep from blushing at

hearing that, even though she wasn't a teenager anymore who would be so easily unnerved by a compliment.

"And trust me," Nicholas said with one of those gorgeous, warm smiles of his, "there isn't anyone else that *I* have the same chemistry with."

Maybe it was the kiss that had spun her around and around so that she couldn't think straight anymore, but instead of finally saying no, she asked, "What will you be filming tomorrow?"

"Kiteboarding."

"I've never done that before." But she'd wanted to.

"Good. I love watching you discover something new. So, would you like to come down and try it? Or," he added with a wicked lift of his eyebrows, "does it not fit into that safe statistical model you have of the world?"

Despite the fact that she knew he was teasing her, she had to know, "Are you calling me a coward?"

"You're one of the strongest, bravest women I've ever met." He moved closer again, close enough that his lips were almost against hers as he said, "And I can't wait to go kiteboarding with you tomorrow."

One quick but oh-so-sweet kiss later, she was left standing alone in the middle of her grandmother's lawn, able to think about nothing but kiteboarding, Nicholas and two kisses that had somehow felt more adventurous—and wonderful—than anything she had ever experienced before.

CHAPTER FOURTEEN

What was she doing?

Rachel had asked herself that question half a dozen times the next morning while she was on her way down to the beach where they'd be filming the next segment. Common sense had dictated that she should stay home, and not just because of the risks involved in kiteboarding.

Because how could so much revolve around Nicholas already when he'd been on the island less than a week? And how could she already care so much? She'd barely been able to sleep the night before because she hadn't been able to stop thinking about his kiss.

It had been so sudden. So perfect. She knew she'd never forget the way Nicholas' lips had tasted. The way his muscles had felt pressed against her. How good he'd smelled, as if he'd just come out of the ocean. And how steady she'd felt when he'd been holding her in his strong arms.

And then, he'd challenged her. Dared her not to say no to this new challenge—obviously knowing she wouldn't be able to turn away from his dare. Especially not when she'd always wondered what it would be like to go kiteboarding.

"Hi, Nicholas," she said as she approached him on the beach. "What do you need me to do for the shoot today?"

He didn't answer right away, simply smiled at her as if he'd never been happier to see anyone in his life. "You'll need a wet suit. After that, I'll run you through the basics of staying on the board and catching the wind with the kite. It's fast and feels a little out of control, but a lot of fun once you get going."

Ever since she'd met Nicholas, Rachel had felt as though her entire life had begun spiraling out of control, moving far too fast. Yet, amazingly, when she didn't overthink everything, it felt right. And she'd definitely had fun, too.

While she changed into the wet suit, her nerves slowly built. They would be going at high speed on open water with nothing but a kite to help them control what they were doing. Hit one wave wrong, catch one gust of wind that wasn't quite right, and the results could be disastrous. She'd looked up the statistics last night, of course. Broken bones, unconsciousness leading to drowning, concussion...there were so many things that could potentially go wrong.

A week ago, Rachel would never have agreed

to do this. Yet now, it felt as if her old instincts had started to come out of a long, dark hibernation. The same feeling of determination she'd had climbing the cliff face was with her right now, telling her to ignore the risks for once.

And the truth was that she *wanted* to do this, even though it was dangerous. She wanted to feel as alive as she had on top of the cliffs with Nicholas.

As alive as she'd felt when he'd kissed her.

"Are you ready?" Nicholas asked. From the way he was watching her, she knew he wasn't just asking about the kiteboarding.

Rachel couldn't have held back her answering smile even if she'd tried. "I'm ready."

They started out slowly and carefully, just the way Nicholas had approached every one of their adventures together. As he showed her how to securely strap herself on to the short board and then how to stand up so that she was balanced, he assured her, "This part isn't quite as hard as when you're surfing, because you've got the force of the kite to brace against. The trick is adjusting to the wind."

It was a relatively calm day, but even so, she could feel the wind ruffling her hair, reminding her of its power. Next, he showed her the proper way to hold the kite and how to use it to catch the wind, explaining that she'd need to learn to feel which way the wind was blowing and then use the gusts that were there rather than trying to force the board to go in the direction she wanted.

It was hard work, but that was also the beauty of it. There was no time to think about anything else while she was out on the water. For the moment, everything came down to the wind and the waves—actually, the wind, the waves *and* Nicholas.

And it was awesome.

He kept pace with her, shouting instructions above the noise of the sea. "You're doing great. Now try turning."

As Rachel followed his directions, the speed of the board was terrifying and incredible all at the same time. She skimmed the tops of the waves until she finally lost the breeze and fell into the water.

She swam back to the support boat and the film crew, then asked, "How was that?"

The camera operator gave her a thumbs-up. "We've got some great shots."

Nicholas hauled himself into the boat just behind her. "You're amazing, Rachel!" The way he was beaming at her told her that he truly meant it.

After they filmed her a few more times, the production assistant asked Nicholas if he could get back into the water alone so that they could film some solo shots where he showed the viewers just what was possible for an expert.

Thrilled to finally get a chance to see him in action, Rachel watched from the boat as he caught the wind and stepped off the boat, skimming straight over the waves as naturally as if he were simply strolling along the street. Running, actually, because he moved fast enough to use the waves like ramps to send him high into the air. The kite became a parachute for the seconds he hung there, giving him time to execute some very impressive spins and flips. He turned and twisted like an acrobat while he was airborne, until it seemed like he couldn't possibly land on his feet. And yet, he did every single time, never even seeming to lose speed.

A split second later, though, the wind caught him, and she gasped as it snapped Nicholas sideways, ripping the board out from under him. He hit the waves at an awkward angle, the board coming free of its safety straps and bouncing up as he slammed into the sea.

Rachel was in the water before she realized what she was doing, swimming out toward Nicholas. What if that board had broken one of his bones or knocked him out? Would she have the strength to drag him back to the waiting boat if he was unconscious?

She would find the strength.

"Nicholas?" She was panting both from swimming so fast and being so frightened for him. "Are you okay?"

"I'm fine." He was holding on to his board and the lines from his kite now. "Come on, let's swim for shore. The boat can follow."

Nicholas swam with the ease and power of someone who had grown up playing in the ocean, and fortunately Rachel had too, so she was able to keep pace. When they finally came up onto the small beach, Rachel could finally see the damage Nicholas' board had done. There was a gash along his arm that might need stitches, but he didn't seem to have any broken bones and was moving easily enough. Thank God.

"It's the board," Nicholas explained. "I designed it with lighter materials and a rounded edge so it's less of a danger when something like this happens."

"You designed it?"

"With the money I earn from competitions and endorsements, I figure why not invest it in designing safer gear for extreme sports?"

Just when she thought he was done surprising her, he did it again. And every time she tried to deny their connection, she was only drawn to him more.

"Thank you for coming in after me," Nicholas said in a grateful voice that made her feel warm all over, despite being soaking wet with cold ocean water. "It really meant a lot to me that you jumped in and swam to me to make sure I was all right."

When she'd thought that Nicholas might be hurt, she had gone to him instinctively. Naturally. And she would do it again in a heartbeat, even though he hadn't needed her to do anything. "You had everything under control."

Nicholas reached out to put a hand over hers. "But it's really nice to know that you were there in case I didn't."

The boat pulled up onto the beach, and as soon as the crew took one look at Nicholas' arm, they declared filming was done for the day. "You need to get to the doctor." Kenny, the camera operator, said. He looked a little green at the sight of blood. "We've got all the shots we need, although we might edit out the last one."

"Actually, I'd appreciate it if you wouldn't," Nicholas said. "People need to see the dangers of what we're doing as well as seeing the fun parts."

"You both were great today," Candice, the production assistant, said. "All three days we've filmed, actually. I'm all but certain that we have everything we need to convince the network that they have a hit show on their hands. So you have my permission to head over to the doctor now."

"You're all heart," Nicholas said with a grin.

* * *

A short while later, Rachel was standing beside Nicholas while he checked in with the nurse at the front desk of the medical center. When Nicholas told her that he'd gotten his injury while kiteboarding, the woman remarked, "That sounds like a very dangerous hobby."

"If you know what you're doing like Nicholas does," Rachel told the nurse, "it's not as bad as you think."

It wasn't long until he was called in to see the doctor, fortunately. Rachel tried to catch up on her work emails on her phone, but she couldn't concentrate. Not when all she could think about was Nicholas.

A short while later, he came back into the waiting room, his arm bandaged and a smile on his face. "Don't we have to pick up Charlotte soon?"

We. He'd just accepted that if Rachel needed to pick up her daughter, then of course he would go with her. Rachel never ceased to be amazed by that. "Charlotte has ballet class today, so Emily drops her at the studio after school, and then Paige brings her back to Grams' house, where she stays and has a girl's night with them all. It's something really special they do together every week."

"Does this mean you have the rest of the day to yourself?"

She should have told him she had work to catch up on. Or at least made *some* excuse for why she couldn't spend more time with him. But Rachel had already spent too much time trying to fight the obvious attraction she felt for Nicholas, and she didn't want to keep fighting anymore. Especially when she'd heard his crew say that they had all the shots they needed. A day, maybe two more, and Nicholas would be gone.

Knowing she'd regret it forever if she missed this one chance to know the joy, and the sweet pleasure, of being with him, she nodded and told him, "And the night, too."

They drove back to her place in silence, then walked hand in hand up to her front step, where he pulled her against him for a kiss. One that was so sweet, and so passionate, it left her hungering for more. *Much* more.

And yet, instead of rushing her into bed, he said, "All along, you've been so determined that this wouldn't happen. Are you sure you want to be with me? Because if you don't, somehow I'll find a way to make myself leave."

It was so sweet that he was concerned for her, but just this once, Rachel didn't want to be careful. If this night was all that they had left, then she wanted to spend it with Nicholas. She wanted to give herself—give both of them—this gift. Something incredibly special to remember.

"If this is going to be our last night, then I want to spend it with you."

"This isn't going to be our last night together," he promised her as he drew her even closer. "Just the first of many."

She kissed him again then, before she could let herself believe in more than just this one night. She knew better, knew how hard it was for some people to stay in one place. One night would be enough. It had to be.

She took hold of his arm, pulling him inside, kissing him again as the door swung shut and she led him back toward her bedroom. It had been so long since she'd let a man be with her like this. So long since she'd dared to make a connection. But, oh, how she wanted to be with him.

And as she kissed him hungrily—and he kissed her right back with just as much need Rachel finally let her self-control go.

CHAPTER FIFTEEN

Rachel woke with Nicholas asleep beside her, his arm curled around her as if to hold on to her for as long as possible. Gently, and with great reluctance, she lifted his arm so that she could get up and shower. Frank wasn't expecting her at the office until later in the day, and Emily would take Charlotte to school from Grams'. Which meant Rachel could take her time, luxuriating in the feel of the water as it hit her skin, all the wonderful memories of the night before making her blush.

Nicholas had been *perfect*. Rachel had expected the night to be good. But it had been more than just their attraction sparking into flames, far more than just one wonderful night with a gorgeous man.

It had felt like they belonged together. As if everything between them ran far deeper than just their physical connection. And by the time they had fallen asleep in one another's arms, it had been hard for Rachel to know where she ended and he began.

By the time she finished showering and went to get dressed in the bedroom, Nicholas was practicing yoga in a pair of board shorts. He straightened when he saw her and smiled. "Good morning."

Yes, she thought as she echoed his greeting, *it certainly is.*

"I have to stretch every morning," he explained, "or I won't be able to do everything I need to on my surfboard. Feel like joining me?"

"From where I'm standing," she replied with a slightly wicked smile on her lips, "watching is working pretty well."

Laughing, Nicholas kept going for another minute or two before putting on a shirt. "Should we head to Ava's to pick up Charlotte for school?"

"Emily will take her in."

"I'll miss seeing her this morning," he said, and she could see that he genuinely meant it, "but in that case, how about I take you out to breakfast?"

"We could have breakfast here," Rachel offered.

"We could, but since I'm guessing you do that every day, let's do something different."

When he reached out to take her hand and led her toward the front door, she could see he wasn't going to take no for an answer. Honestly, Rachel didn't mind. It had been so long since she'd eaten out anywhere, and for breakfast? Had she even done that since Charlotte had been born? Rachel tended to leave spontaneous things for later in the day. So much later that they often didn't happen.

"I'm trusting you," he said as they began to walk into town, "to steer us away from any tourist places. I want to experience what it's like to truly be a local."

"I knew you wanted me for something," Rachel replied with a laugh.

"I want you for a lot more than that," Nicholas assured her.

And it certainly seemed true that he wanted her for a lot more than just a handy local guide to the island. She still could hardly believe the way it had all happened. If Morgan hadn't been ill, Nicholas would have just been some stranger in Grams' house, busy with his TV shoots and then gone as quickly as he'd arrived. Instead, they'd had a wonderful few days together, Rachel had been given the opportunity to revisit some of the excitement she'd had when she was a kid, and Charlotte was happier than ever.

As for last night? Rachel would always be grateful for the precious hours she'd spent in Nicholas' arms.

Just like he liked to say, things *had* worked out. For the time being at least.

In town, Nicholas pointed out the really cool sign of a local art studio that featured a couple of whales chasing each other. How had she not noticed it before? Well, for today at least, she was really enjoying the sights and sounds of the island waking up. The artists coming out into the morning sun to check the light and set up their easels. The tourists starting to get out and explore the island, cameras in hand, eyes bright with anticipation. A couple of fishermen hauling in their early morning catch. It had all been here before, but she felt like she was seeing it for the first time.

"This is so nice," she said softly, loving the feel of her hand in his as they walked.

"I love walking around exploring the places where I surf," Nicholas said. "I've never understood people on the surfing circuit who just go from the airport to the beach and back again when they could be slowing down and enjoying things."

"After seeing you kitesurfing yesterday," Rachel said with a smile, "it's hard to imagine you slowing down. Especially when there's always another wave coming."

Nicholas reached out with his free hand to brush a lock of hair back from her cheek and slide it behind her ear. She was tingling all over by the time he replied. "Hanging out in the deep water without being in any rush until a great wave finally comes along, and then enjoying riding it for as long as you can, is actually what surfing is all about."

"But what about when you're surfing competitively and the good waves don't seem to be coming?"

"It isn't always easy to be patient while you wait for something amazing to come along, but in my experience, it's always worth it. And always loads of fun, too."

For so long, she'd been so busy with work, Charlotte and family, that her life had become one long loop on a never-ending replay. But ever since Nicholas had arrived, she hadn't known from one day to the next what life would throw at her. It should have been terrifying. In fact, there *had* been a couple of moments when it had been terrifying. But there had been far more moments when excitement—and pleasure—had overridden everything else.

For the past several years, she had defined herself as "responsible," "safety conscious" and "a super protective mom." And she knew these were the same terms anyone else would use to describe her. But hadn't she known all along that there was more to her than those descriptors? Even if, for the past few years, she had been living a life that was the polar opposite of being a cliff-climbing adventurer.

"What about this place?" Nicholas asked, gesturing to a small café close to the waterfront. "Is this how the locals do breakfast?"

Rachel hadn't been in this café in years. It looked just the same as it had when she was a teenager and used to stay out until the sun was starting to rise, or when she'd wanted to grab a quick breakfast on the way to the beach.

"Yes," she said, "this place is really good."

Everything was as Rachel remembered it, from the checkered tablecloths to the aging coffee machine. Even the girl behind the counter looked familiar, and Rachel guessed she was the daughter of the woman who had owned the café when she was a kid.

"What do you recommend?" Nicholas asked.

"Honestly, it's all really good. I think I'm going to have the pancakes and bacon."

Just then, everything felt right. Even the weather was perfect, one of the beautiful, sunny, but not too hot, mornings that Walker Island was famous for. And the pancakes and bacon were as good as she remembered.

"How about later, after you get back from work and Charlotte is done with school, the three of us go down to the beach and I'll show you both how to surf?"

Rachel thought back to her daughter trying to "surf" on the ironing board, and her stomach clenched tight. "Isn't she too young?"

"I was a lot younger when I first got on a board," Nicholas pointed out. "But I wouldn't want you to feel uncomfortable about her safety, so if you'd rather learn first, then after you've got it down, both of us could teach—"

Rachel's chest had clenched even tighter by the time she raised a hand to stop him from saying anything more. "Can we not do this?"

"Not do what?"

"Not make plans like this."

"I thought you liked making plans. I mean, I'm

usually happy to go with the flow and just see what happens, because things always end up working out, but—"

"Sometimes they *don't* work out!" Rachel hated the way their perfect morning had turned so quickly. "You keep talking about all the things that we're going to do next, but I know exactly what's happening next. You're *leaving*. You've finished your shooting for the pilot and we can't pretend that you'll be able to stay in one place, even if you had a reason to stay."

"I *do* have a reason to stay," Nicholas insisted, reaching for her hand. "Two wonderful reasons. Even more, actually, when we count your family. I want this, Rachel. I want *you*."

Rachel pulled back, not because she didn't want the touch of his skin against hers, but because she wanted it far *too* much. "You have too much going on in your life to stay here. You have your new TV show. You have your surfing competitions around the world. Because I don't think they're planning on holding all the major surfing championships around Walker Island this year, are they?"

"It probably wouldn't make for particularly great waves," Nicholas said with one of his gentle smiles. "But that doesn't mean we have to just pull back like nothing happened last night or pretend we can't still feel the sparks between us."

"Last night was wonderful, but I knew going into it that it was only going to be the one night we had together. I knew that you were leaving, and I—" She took a deep breath, one that shook inside her chest. "I didn't want to regret never taking that chance to be with you."

"And do you regret it?" Nicholas asked, his hand finding hers and holding on tight.

"No. How could I? It was beautiful. So, so beautiful." Rachel could feel the tears coming now and knew she needed to finish this conversation soon, before they spilled out in front of Nicholas. "I know I can't stop you from leaving, and I wouldn't want to. Your life's one that should be lived throughout the world, away from this island. All I wanted was to be part of it, even if just for a short time."

"We could build so many other memories together," Nicholas insisted. "We don't have to call an end to this. To us."

"Even if you stayed for a few more days, it wouldn't make things better. Because you'd still have to leave in the end." The tears came even closer as she told him, "That's why I think it would be easier for both of us—and for Charlotte, so that she doesn't get any more attached to you—if you leave today."

"Come with me."

She blinked at him in shock for several moments, before finally echoing, "Come with you?"

"Yes. Come with me," he said again, as if it were the most obvious idea in the world. "I've seen the way you come to life when you're having fun on our adventures. And I see the way

Charlotte longs for adventure, too. Why not get on a plane with me and see the world?"

Rachel continued to stare at him in disbelief. He had to be joking, didn't he?

But no. It looked like Nicholas was deadly serious.

"That's crazy."

"What's crazy about it?" Nicholas countered.

"*Everything!* I know what your schedule is like, what's going to be next. Australia. Japan. Thailand. You're talking like I can just get up and walk away from my life here. Like I don't have responsibilities. But I have a little girl and a job that I need so that I can keep a roof over our heads and food in our stomachs. You can't be serious about dragging Charlotte around the world like that!"

But Nicholas didn't let go of her hand. "I'm completely serious. Are you telling me that you love your job so much you couldn't leave it? And as for Charlotte, from what I hear, homeschooling is a pretty awesome thing. I'm not asking you to abandon her. I would never want that, not for any of us. I want her to come, too. All three of us, going everywhere we want. As a family." His eyes were intense with emotion as he told her, "You asked me the other day if I'd ever wanted a family." He lifted her fingers to his mouth and pressed a kiss to them. "I want you and Charlotte to be my family. Can't you see what an amazing life we could have together?"

Rachel was stunned by how easily she could

imagine it. Going to parts of the world she'd always wanted to visit. Traveling with Charlotte and Nicholas beside her to exotic locations her daughter would love. Teaching Charlotte from home. Not spending her days poring over insurance statistics, because instead she would be filming shows with Nicholas. And, best of all, getting to wake up in his arms every morning.

It was tempting. *So* incredibly tempting to reach for the beautiful dream.

But, she forcefully reminded herself, a dream was all it was. There were way too many risks. What if Nicholas changed his mind? What if he realized that being tied down with a woman and her kid wasn't everything he'd expected? What about all the difficulties that might come with taking a little girl away from the only home she'd ever known?

"I'm sorry, Nicholas," Rachel said. "I can't take that kind of risk. Not when it comes to Charlotte."

And especially not when it came to her own heart...

CHAPTER SIXTEEN

During the walk back to her grandmother's place, Rachel kept telling herself that she'd done exactly what she'd needed to do. After all, Charlotte's well-being came before everything. And if Nicholas couldn't see that, then it was even *more* obvious that they couldn't be together.

But that had been obvious from the moment he'd arrived, hadn't it? Yes, they'd had a connection, but it had always been a connection with an expiration date. Even last night, she'd gone into it with her eyes open, knowing that Nicholas would be leaving today. Making love with him had been about saying good-bye, not about the beginning of forever. And she'd been sure that Nicholas would eventually accept that, too, even if he kept wanting to talk about the future.

When she walked into Gram's house, she found her daughter in the kitchen, along with

Paige and Grams. Charlotte jumped up when she saw her, giving her a big hug.

"What happened?" Rachel said when she saw the small bandage on her daughter's knee.

"I was dancing. Doing spins."

"It's nothing serious," Paige reassured her. "Just a skinned knee. You were very brave, weren't you, Charlotte?"

"She always is," Rachel said with a smile, one that wobbled a little. "The bravest little girl in the world."

Paige took a closer look at her. "Are you okay, Rachel? It's really not that bad of a scratch. I'd have called you if it had been serious."

"No, it's not that. It's Nicholas."

"What about Nicholas, Mommy?"

Rachel did her best to smile again, even though inside she was absolutely falling to pieces. She'd been hoping that if she didn't mention Nicholas in front of Charlotte, her daughter would come to terms more quickly with the idea of him going away. Now that she'd accidentally blown it, they were probably in for some tears. From both of them...

"I'm sorry, sweetie," she said as she knelt down to her daughter's level, "but Nicholas has to go away."

"But I don't want him to," Charlotte insisted.

"I know you don't"—*and neither do I*—"but..."

When her voice started to break, Paige gently reached out to take her niece's hand. "We need to leave for school now so that you're not late.

Especially when you have finger-painting first thing today and I know how much you love it."

Thankfully, Paige's reminder of finger-painting helped Charlotte temporarily forget about Nicholas leaving. After Rachel gave her daughter a hug and a kiss good-bye, Grams sat down at the kitchen table and gestured for Rachel to do the same.

"What's all this about Nicholas? Did you and he have a fight?"

Rachel stared at her grandmother in disbelief. "You make it sound like we're a couple."

"Aren't you?"

"No," she said, but it felt like a lie. "Well, maybe it felt like we had started to become one after we..." She paused a beat, before deciding to spill everything. "After we slept together."

Her grandmother smiled. "I guessed that part. We would have been blind not to see the sparks between the two of you the other night at dinner."

She should have known Grams wouldn't be surprised, let alone shocked. After all, she'd been the one who had talked Rachel into coming back home to Walker Island after Guy left. Her grandmother had always been so good at dealing with the ever-changing love lives of her five granddaughters.

"So is that it?" Grams asked. "You slept with him and you think you made a mistake?"

Rachel shook her head. Sleeping with Nicholas couldn't ever be a mistake. Not when it had been the most beautiful night of her life.

"Then what?" Grams prompted. "You know you can share this with me, darling. Tell me what's wrong and why you look so sad."

"I was all prepared for him to leave, but then he told me that he wanted us to go with him." The words couldn't come fast enough now that she was finally letting them spill out. "He had this crazy scheme in his head that I would give up my job, homeschool Charlotte, and we'd go with him to wherever the next adventure is."

"And you're angry at him for that?"

"He just expects that everything will work out, and it clearly always has for him. But that's not the way the real world works. Not for me anyway."

Grams reached out to take her hand. "You have a beautiful daughter and a family that loves you. Has it really all worked out so badly?"

"No, of course not. I love Charlotte. I love all of you, too. You know that. But when he asked me to go with him this morning, it felt like he was trying to coax me up some cliff face with promises of what might lie ahead, even though there aren't any safety ropes to catch us if something happens. It felt like he was asking me to throw our whole lives away for the sake of some unknown adventures that might, or might not, work out."

"Perhaps," Grams gently suggested, "he didn't see it like that. Maybe he thought he was offering you more. Maybe he thought he was helping to make not only his own dreams come true, but yours, too." That stopped Rachel in her tracks for a long moment, especially when Grams asked, "Are you telling me there wasn't a part of you that was tempted?"

Of course there had been. At least until she'd started worrying about all the things that might go wrong...

"You sound almost like you're on his side, Grams."

"I'm on your side. Always." Grams reached for her hand. "When you were a little girl, you got into so many scrapes because you were utterly fearless. After your mother died, I know you often used adventure as a way to escape—and that perhaps you went a little too far sometimes—but before that, you used to climb anything, run anywhere and dive into anything just for *fun*. Simply because you *loved* the adventure of it all. More than any of the rest of us, you loved experiencing new things and testing your limits to see all the amazing things you were capable of achieving."

"Maybe," Rachel said slowly as she tried to let everything her grandmother was saying sink in, "that was because I didn't know enough about the consequences back then."

"Or maybe," Grams countered, "it was because you knew the joy you'd feel was more than worth taking the risk?" She smiled as she remembered. "Practically every time the school called, it was the nurse saying you'd bumped your head or skinned your knees again. It's a wonder that you still had knees by the end of it all. But when I'd arrive to collect you, you'd be sitting in the nurse's office with a smile on your face, ready to tell me all about what you'd tried to do and how you were going to get it right next time."

At the mention of skinned knees, Rachel thought about the fall Charlotte had taken while twirling around and around at the dance studio. When she had seen the bandage, her heart had briefly jumped into her mouth. She'd been so worried about her little girl. Yet, Charlotte had seemed perfectly happy, hadn't she? As if she expected to fall sometimes while having fun, and that it was okay, just as long as she always got right back up and tried again.

"I know you're worried about taking Charlotte away from the island, and obviously, I want to see as much of you both as I can, but I also want my girls to have the kind of lives they truly deserve. Charlotte is as fearless as you were, Rachel. You know that. You've always known it. Don't you want her to grow up being confident about enjoying life to the fullest?"

"Of course I do," Rachel said, "but I wish—" She shook her head. "I know I can't protect her from everything, especially not a broken heart, no matter how much I wish I could."

"You know how dangerous everything is, darling, but you seem to have forgotten about how joyous and beautiful it all is, as well. You once told me when you were a teenager that it's worth risking falling to get to the top of a cliff."

Grams squeezed Rachel's hand tight. "That's just as true now as it was back then. And I can promise you that when Charlotte lands that spin she was practicing, it will be worth even more to her because she fell a few times along the way."

"But taking a chance on leaving with Nicholas isn't just about learning a dance move," Rachel pointed out.

"No, it has the potential to be much more than that. And as a dancer, you can imagine I don't say that very often. Now," Grams said with a kiss to her forehead, "I think both of us could do with a nice, hot cup of coffee."

Was Grams right? Had Rachel let herself become so scared of the potential consequences of life that she wouldn't let herself enjoy the things that mattered? Of course, all she had to do was look at how much more alive she'd felt this week to know the answer. Every time Nicholas had persuaded her to take a risk, she had felt more and more like the real her.

Yet even so, could she really do this?

When her grandmother brought her over a mug of steaming coffee, instead of taking a sip, she said, "I want so badly to believe things will always work out, but look at what happened with Guy. And with Mom."

"I know Guy hurt you, but once you learned exactly what he was—or rather, *wasn't*—made of, don't you think that both you and Charlotte were better off without him?" After Rachel nodded, Grams said, "And what happened to your mother was a terrible tragedy, but do you think for one moment that she would have wanted you to pull back and not live your life because of it? You've become such a strong, independent woman and a wonderful mother without Guy. Now, you just need to let yourself take a few risks so that you can learn what truly makes you happy."

"But this isn't just about me, it's about Charlotte, too."

"And we both know that going off on adventures around the world would be a dream come true for her, just as I know that you will do a wonderful job of bringing her up, no matter where you are. The question is, what do *you* want?" Grams held her gaze. "Do you love Nicholas? Would this be a dream come true for you, too?"

Yes, it would. Rachel knew without having to look very hard that traveling around the world with Nicholas and Charlotte would be everything she'd ever wanted. She could see how it might work, but...

"I'm scared, Grams."

"Being scared is good," Ava said with a smile. "Stopping because you're scared is not. When I persuaded you to come back to the island after Guy disappeared, it wasn't so that you could hide away from the world. It was so that you could build up your strength to fly out there again. And you know that we'll always be here to catch you and Charlotte if you should ever fall. That's what family is for."

"Thank you so much, Grams," Rachel said as she threw her arms around her grandmother's shoulders. "You're the best! Now I need to go find Nicholas."

"I'm very glad to hear it," Grams said, looking as pleased as she ever had. "Although you might have to hurry. His film crew came to collect some of his things a little while ago, and I think they were heading down to the harbor."

CHAPTER SEVENTEEN

Rachel sprinted out of the house. Her home was closer than the docks, meaning that her car was too, but was it close enough? But there was no time for her to calculate everything carefully. Not now.

Not where Nicholas was concerned.

She dashed toward her house, deciding that the car would be fastest. At least the way she was going to drive today, it would be. Running up the sidewalk, she narrowly avoided crashing into a couple of tourists taking in the sights, then took a shortcut down a small alleyway and hopped over a low wall. A dog barked at her, and Rachel ran faster, getting back out onto the street. She hadn't done anything like this since she used to run home from school as a kid.

She skidded to a halt across the street from her house. For once, the street was busy, cars coming one after another. She tried to be patient, waiting at the curbside, but then she shook her head. "There isn't any time."

And there wasn't. Every second she spent waiting for the perfectly safe time to cross, the film crew would be getting closer to the docks with Nicholas. She couldn't stand the thought of him leaving thinking that she didn't care—or that she wasn't ready to change her whole life for him.

All along, he'd opened up his heart, and his life, to her. Now that she was finally ready to do the same, she prayed she wasn't too late.

When was the next ferry due to leave? The big car ferries departed every hour, but the smaller passenger boats that tied up on the jetties often went more often than that. She needed to hurry!

Rachel checked her watch, took a breath and then stepped out into the traffic. "Sorry, sorry!" she called out as horns blared, but she kept moving. As she pulled open her garage door, she wished she owned a sports car that would get her there in half the time than the Kia could. Maybe a motorcycle. That would let her easily cut through the small town's traffic, wouldn't it?

She pulled out into the street, then took her car up to the speed limit and past it as she pulled around a couple of cyclists on the narrow island road, cutting back in quickly to avoid oncoming traffic.

"Everything will be okay," Rachel said to herself, trying to calm down, working to convince herself that she would get there before Nicholas left. Things would work out, the way he always said they did. She would *make* them work out!

Could she call Hanna and get her to persuade Joel to stop the ferry, given that he owned the company? It was worth a try—anything was at this point—so she used the voice-activated dialing on her cell phone. Unfortunately, she only got through to voice mail. "Hi, Hanna, it's Rachel. Listen, if you get this in the next few minutes, I need Joel to delay the next ferry off the island for as long as possible. I'll explain later, but it's important. You know I wouldn't ask otherwise. Love you, bye!"

Rachel hung up and concentrated on driving. The roads on Walker Island weren't designed for high-speed driving. They were meant for meandering along while looking at the sights. Nicholas had reminded her of that when he'd walked with her earlier, making her slow down enough to notice the beauty all around her again.

Finally at the crowded harbor, she left the car in a no-parking zone and ran again, dodging a group of fishermen and the group of tourists photographing them. Several marine biologists were loading up a small boat, and not far from them a man and a woman were tuning up their Jet Skis.

Rachel hurdled a small stack of equipment and drew to a halt at the spot where the ferry normally tied up, but it wasn't there.

Oh no, this couldn't be right! It wasn't the way things were supposed to happen now that she'd finally found a wonderful man who cared for both her and Charlotte.

She went over to the ticket booth and breathlessly asked, "The ferry to the mainland, has it gone yet?"

"One left a couple of minutes ago."

Rachel couldn't believe it. She'd tried so hard to get here quickly, but it looked like she was too late. Unless...

"Was there a film crew on the boat?" Maybe they'd missed the ferry just like she had or had decided to stop in a cafe for a meal first before leaving the island.

"Yes, I remember them. They had loads of boxes and cameras and a surfboard, too."

Oh no, that meant Nicholas *was* on the ferry. Gone, just like that. But she wouldn't give up this time, couldn't stand to let Nicholas leave without knowing just how much she loved him.

Because she did. She *loved* him. With her entire heart and soul.

And she would prove it to him, even if it was the scariest thing she'd ever done.

Rachel ran up to the marine biologists. "I really need to catch up to the ferry that just left. Can I borrow your boat? I grew up on the island, so I promise I know how to operate a speedboat."

"Borrow our boat? Are you nuts?"

"No, I promise you, I'm not. But I really need to catch up to the ferry."

"And we need to get on with our research," the scientist countered.

"I can pay you." It was desperate, but then, so was Rachel.

The biologist only shook his head. "I'm afraid this isn't a pleasure cruiser. You'll have to find someone else or wait for the next ferry."

But she couldn't wait, so she immediately headed toward the jet-skiing couple just a few yards away. They were both in their late teens. The young man was dressed in board shorts, while the young woman was wearing cutoffs and a bikini top. They both had the tanned, athletic frames of people who spent most of their time out on the water having fun, and they reminded her of herself at that age.

Only, it wasn't a painful memory anymore. Because the past wasn't the point. The future was.

Nicholas was.

"I know this is going to sound weird, but I need to catch up with the ferry that just left here. Please, could you take me out to it?"

"Hey," the girl said, "aren't you one of the Walkers?"

"Yes, I'm Rachel Walker."

"Cool. I'm Iona Bledsoe. Your dad taught my English classes in high school, and I used to go for dance classes down at your grandmother's studio. Why do you want to catch up to the ferry?"

"Because the man I love is on it, and if I don't tell him today, he's probably going to go away forever. Please, can you help me?"

"For true love, absolutely! Hey, Jake, throw her your life vest, would you?" Thankfully, the girl's boyfriend immediately complied, at which point Iona said, "Climb on behind me."

Rachel clung tightly to Iona as they shot away from the jetty. The fact that the speed they were going ended up dousing the marine biologists in their precious boat was just a happy bonus.

The water in the harbor was quite still today, but with so many boats around, it was still a hair-raising experience as the Jet Ski zipped and darted around obstacles, heading for the open sea.

"There it is!" Rachel yelled above the sound of the motor.

They went faster then, skimming the tops of rolling waves that were probably too big to be safe for such a small vessel. Yet, right then, she didn't care as the wind whipped through her hair, along with the cold sea spray. All that mattered was catching up with Nicholas before he disappeared completely.

Thankfully, the ferry wasn't moving that fast. Certainly not as fast as the Jet Ski could go at full throttle. And, thankfully, Iona didn't mind giving the chase everything she could.

"So, what's the plan when we get there?" Iona yelled back to her.

"Just get alongside and try to match the boat's speed so that I can call out to the people on board to get Nicholas' attention."

Soon, Iona was bringing the Jet Ski alongside the ferry, holding it steady. Even so, on the open sea "steady" was a relative term. Several tourists and islanders looked over the side of the ferry, obviously wondering if Rachel had lost her mind as she yelled, "Is Nicholas Quinn on board? I need to talk to him."

After a few seconds, Candice, the production assistant, ran out to the ferry's deck and yelled, "What are you doing here, Rachel?"

"I need to talk to Nicholas."

The woman looked shocked. "You sped all the way out here on a Jet Ski just to talk to him?"

"Please," Rachel yelled, "can you tell him I'm here?"

"I would, but he isn't on board. He said he couldn't leave the island yet. He told us he had something really important that he needed to do, something about 'proving it can work,' though he wouldn't tell us anything more than that. I'm really sorry, Rachel."

But Rachel wasn't sorry at all. Not anymore, not when it sounded like Nicholas was still utterly intent on a life with her and Charlotte. Just as much as they wanted a life with him.

"How fast do you think you can get us back to the docks?" Rachel asked Iona.

Instead of replying, the other woman was already gunning the motor, speeding them back across the ocean again as fast as the Jet Ski could go.

All in the name of true love.

CHAPTER EIGHTEEN

Nicholas stepped inside the island's high school, and kids quickly began pointing at him as they realized who he was. But he wasn't going to be able to stop to chat or sign autographs for any of them today, because he needed to speak with Emily Walker right away.

Was he doing the right thing?

Not about Rachel. That part couldn't be more clear. He loved her. He wanted to be with her, whatever that took. The question was whether he was doing the right thing by coming to see her sister without discussing it with Rachel first.

But he knew Rachel needed facts, figures and the kind of certainty about homeschooling Charlotte that Nicholas could only give her if he talked to her school counselor sister first. This wasn't about presenting Rachel with a fait accompli. It was about showing her that the choice he was asking her to make to change her and her daughter's lives could work.

Emily's office door was open when he got there, thankfully. Noting that she was looking out over the school's football field where practice was taking place, he asked, "Are you a football fan?"

When she turned toward him, it occurred to him yet again that while each of the Walker sisters was beautiful, only Rachel made him feel that fierce spark of love and desire.

"You can't live on Walker Island and *not* be a football fan. But today I'm thinking more about how nice it would be to be outside rather than in my office."

"I'm sorry about keeping you late. Thank you for agreeing to see me."

"I would have been here late anyway." Emily easily waved off his apology as she shut the door behind them and then gestured for him to sit down. "The real question is, what are *you* still doing here?"

"Was everyone in your family expecting me to take the first ferry off the island as soon as I could?" He'd sent his gear on ahead with the film crew, but he couldn't leave. Not when everything he'd ever wanted, everything he longed for, was still here.

She raised an eyebrow at his question as she sat behind her desk. "We're all just looking out for my sister."

"It's great the way you take care of each other," he said, before gently adding, "but you know Rachel can look out for herself, don't you?"

"Of course I do," Emily replied, "but knowing that doesn't stop you from being protective when you care about someone."

"It doesn't," he agreed. He already felt incredibly protective toward both Rachel and Charlotte and knew he always would, because he loved them both.

She gave him a small smile. "Why don't you tell me what's on your mind, Nicholas? I've got as long as you need."

It was easy to see what a great guidance counselor she must be—Emily was ready to listen and help. She also clearly wanted the best for her sister, just as the rest of their family did. Which meant that it wouldn't be a good idea to do anything to hurt Rachel or Charlotte. Not unless he wanted the whole Walker clan coming after him.

Of course, he would never want to hurt them. Not in a million years.

"I'm in love with Rachel."

"Tell me something I don't know," Emily said with a wide grin. "After working in a high school for so long—and having four younger sisters—I can tell when two people are falling in love from a mile away."

Nicholas thought about Michael. Did Emily have any idea that he'd been madly in love with her for years? But he had more sense than to say anything. Right now he needed Emily's help, not to get her back up by interfering in her love life.

"So if you're in love with my sister," she said,

"does that mean that you're going to be staying on the island?"

"If I thought that was what Rachel really wanted, I'd do it." And if, in the end, staying here truly was what Rachel and Charlotte needed him to do, he would reduce his surfing competitions and other travel commitments. For them, it would be worth it to change his entire life.

"You don't think Rachel wants to stay on the island?"

He wasn't surprised by her slightly defensive tone. Not when he'd seen how much Emily loved Walker Island and how much she loved having her sisters close by.

"Of course she loves the island, but I think Rachel has only stayed here because it feels like the safer option," he explained. "I saw the way she came alive every time we were out on the water or climbing during filming. She loves adventure, but has been smothering it because she believes that's the only way to do the right thing for Charlotte."

"There are plenty of adventures to have here on the island," Emily insisted.

"I agree. And I promise you I'm not attacking Walker Island. It's a beautiful place to grow up, and to live, but there's so much else out there. So much that I want to share with Rachel and Charlotte. So much that I know the two of them would love to discover with me. Do you really think that she's happy here, working as an actuary? Because as far as I can see, the only things in her life that truly make her smile are her family and Charlotte."

And *him*. He'd made Rachel happy. Just as happy as she'd made him.

For a few moments, Emily looked like she was about to argue with him. But then she suddenly said, "You're right." She sighed. "I know you're right. Rachel hasn't been truly happy since she moved back to the island. We've all tried to be there for her, but it's like one version of her went out into the world, and another one came back. When she was a kid, she was so adventurous. We used to argue sometimes because I thought she was being irresponsible, setting a bad example for our younger sisters. But now I see that she was just having fun. Being who she needed to be. Maybe she overdid it a little sometimes, but all teenagers do at some point." She paused for a moment, looking pensive, before she continued. "After our mom died, she became even more adventurous and wild. But then, when she got pregnant and came back to the island, she ended up swinging all the way to the other extreme, always so concerned with making sure everything was safe. Never wanting to take a risk at all. It was as if the adventurous woman inside of her was just...gone."

"It's not gone," Nicholas assured her. "Trust me, if you'd seen her face when she was climbing the cliffs with me, you'd know that. From the very first moment I met her, I saw a smart, exciting, adventurous woman. Yes, she wants to know that she and Charlotte are going to be okay, but any mother would feel that way. Especially one as devoted to her daughter as she is."

Emily looked closely at him. It was a look that reminded Nicholas of being in the principal's office as a kid, about to receive a lecture on not surfing so long that he forgot to come to school on time. "*Will* my sister and niece come out of this okay?"

"I love both of them. Which is why I'm here to learn more about homeschooling so that I can show Rachel that Charlotte will not only be okay, but will thrive."

Emily stared at him for a long moment, as if to fully take his measure. Finally, she smiled and reached into a large desk drawer, pulling out some brochures and some printed sheets she'd obviously put together herself.

"There are a lot of requirements and forms. Deciding to homeschool is a big commitment. It's recommended that both you and Rachel take a parent qualifying course."

Nicholas kept listening as he read through the top set of papers. It was indeed a complicated process, but honestly, was it any more complicated than the design development at his company when they were trying to come up with better safety equipment? There were always plenty of tests, forms and legal requirements to fulfill, and the well-being of Rachel's daughter was far more important than anything else.

"Of course," Emily said, "there are things like

setting curricula, deciding what to teach and when. And you'd still have to meet with accredited teachers regularly to make sure things are on track. Which is where it helps that my father is a teacher."

"Don't worry, we will come back here often," he replied to her unspoken question. "And not just to check in with your father about our homeschooling progress. I promise that I'm not trying to take your sister or niece away forever. I'm just trying to give Rachel and Charlotte the kind of lives they would love."

"I know," Emily said with another smile, one that told him she was now as sure of him as she needed to be. "I've put together all the details you're going to need to get started. Would you like me to help you draw up a plan?"

"Thank you, but I think Rachel and I should create Charlotte's homeschooling plan together."

When it had just been him, he often went off to his next event without planning anything, knowing that he would find somewhere to stay and that the surfing competition would work out great, too. Now there would be all kinds of considerations to take into account, from declarations of intent to homeschool to more basic things, like how the three of them were going to get to his next competition or filming location together. They would need to find time to teach Charlotte, but again, that wasn't a problem. If anything, Nicholas had a better lifestyle for that than someone trying to work a nine-to-five job. They would also have to sort out things like making sure Rachel and Charlotte had passports, planning an itinerary, and working out where to stay in each new part of the world.

There were no problems that were insurmountable, as far as Nicholas could see. Better than that, there were no problems that he couldn't prove were easily solvable. Having Rachel take it on trust was great, but being able to actually show her that it would be fine was even better.

Responsibility had crept up on him when he wasn't looking...and the best part was that he was totally okay with that. More than okay with it, actually, he thought with a big smile. It felt right.

Completely right.

Emily's phone rang, and when she looked at the name on the screen and smiled, he knew exactly who was calling even before she picked up and said, "Rachel, I was just thinking about you."

At the sound of Rachel's name, Nicholas wanted to leap up and take the phone out of Emily's hand so that he could tell her—again—how much he loved her.

"Hold on, you did what?" Emily looked a little stunned, then pleased, as she listened to her sister's response. "Wow, it sounds like you've had quite a day, haven't you?" She paused to listen again, then nodded. "No problem, you shouldn't have to wait too long. Bye."

"Is Rachel okay?" he asked the moment Emily

hung up.

"I think that depends on your definition of okay," Emily said with a shake of her head, but he could tell she was still more than a little pleased by whatever had transpired. "She was just telling me a story about chasing after the ferry on a Jet Ski—all because she thought you were leaving."

Rachel had come after him!

Relief—and joy—were both coursing through his veins as Emily continued. "And then, when she found out you weren't on the ferry, she called Morgan to see if you were with her in the TV studio. Our sister didn't pick up, so Rachel was heading there in her car in the hopes that Morgan was filming and had turned her phone off. Halfway to Morgan's place, one of her tires gave out. She just asked me to pick Charlotte up from school first, and then get her from the side of the road where she's waiting." Emily reached into her pocket for a set of keys and handed them to him.

"You're really okay with me going to pick up your niece and your sister? You'd trust me to do that?"

The smile Emily gave him was bright and warm, with no more of the wariness in her eyes that he'd seen when he'd first walked into her office. "Honestly, I don't think there's anyone I'd trust more at this point. And more importantly, I know there's no one Rachel would trust more. I'll call Charlotte's teacher to let her know you'll be picking her up. After that, you know the way from here to Morgan's house so that you'll actually be able to find my sister?"

"Rachel is the woman I've been looking for my entire life. Don't worry," he promised, "I'll find her."

CHAPTER NINETEEN

Rachel stood by her car, still more than a little stunned that she'd been felled at the same spot for a second time. She'd known about the pothole, but she'd been in such a hurry to get to Morgan's studio to see if Nicholas was there, that she'd forgotten about it until it was too late.

As she stood on the side of the road again and stared at yet another flat tire—one she couldn't even fix this time because she hadn't yet had a chance to replace the spare after the first flat—she couldn't help but think about how different she felt today compared to the day she'd met Nicholas when she'd popped her tire on the way to pick him up from the ferry.

She'd been wary at first. Then attracted, despite herself. And now, she was in love.

Wholly, totally, completely in love.

Which was why she needed Emily and Charlotte to get here soon so they could track down Nicholas—and she could finally tell him what was in her heart. She knew she could have called him and told him over the phone, but she wanted to be able to look into his eyes when she told him. And she wanted him to be able to read her boundless love for him in her expression, too.

Hearing the sound of an engine, Rachel was extremely glad to look up and see Emily's car. But as the car came closer, she was surprised to see that it wasn't her sister behind the wheel.

It was Nicholas.

Her heart was leaping as the car pulled to a stop. Oh, how she loved him. And how she wanted him to know it. But before she could get to him, Charlotte got out of the car and barreled toward her.

"Mommy, Nicholas came and got me from school!" Charlotte's arms came around Rachel's middle and held on tight. "He said we had to look for you on the side of the road, and I spotted you first!"

"I'm so glad you found me, sweetie." She drew her daughter into her arms and held her tight. "I'm so glad *both* of you found me."

Nicholas moved forward then, and when he put his arms around both of them, nothing had ever felt more right.

Only one thing could have made it better.

"I love you, Rachel."

He had no idea how much she'd needed to hear those words again. Just to know that they were still true. And that she hadn't blown her chance to be with him.

She stared into his beautiful eyes and finally told him what was in her heart. "I love you, too. So, so much."

"I guessed that when I heard about the Jet Ski," he said with a wide, and very impressed, smile.

Rachel smiled back just as big. "I wasn't going to let you go without a fight."

Charlotte kept a hold on them both as she asked, "What did you do with a Jet Ski, Mommy?"

Rachel looked down at her daughter, smiling. "I went for a ride on one because I thought Nicholas was going away." She looked back up at Nicholas, letting all the love she felt for him shine through as she said, "And I really didn't want him to go."

"Nicholas wasn't going away," her daughter replied as if it was the most obvious thing in the world that he'd be there for both of them. "He was getting me from school."

Rachel moved to kneel next to her daughter. "Charlotte, I know you love living here on the island, but what do you think about the two of us joining Nicholas on his adventures around the world?"

"Would we get to go on airplanes?"

"Yes," Rachel replied, "and trains and buses and boats, too."

"Would I still get to see everyone? Grams and Grandpa and Aunt Emily and Paige and Morgan and Hanna?"

Kneeling beside Rachel, Nicholas said, "Absolutely. We'll come back for lots and lots of visits."

Charlotte asked Nicholas, "Will you teach me how to surf?"

Rachel ran a hand over her daughter's soft hair. "I'm sure he will. And I'm sure you'll be brilliant at learning how to do it. We both will."

Charlotte beamed at her. "Okay."

It must be wonderful being six, Rachel decided, when life really was that simple. Although right then, everything seemed pretty perfect for her, too. She wanted to be with Nicholas...and he wanted to be with her and Charlotte.

"Are you and Nicholas going to kiss now, Mommy?"

Rachel nodded. "I hope so."

"Kissing is icky." Charlotte made a face. Apparently, the thought of kissing boys still hadn't lost its *ew* factor for her, Rachel thought as she moved more closely into Nicholas' outstretched arms.

She let herself enjoy the feel of his strong, warm arms around her for a few wondering moments before she said, "Soon, you'll have to tell me all about how you came to be picking Charlotte and me up in Emily's car rather than my sister. But first—"

She tipped her chin up for a kiss just as he lowered his mouth to hers for a sweet yet sexy kiss that had her longing for more than just one.

She didn't even care when a horn sounded behind them and a car shot past with teenagers whooping at the sight of them kissing in public.

Pure love was written all over Nicholas' face as he told her, "I went to see Emily to ask for information on homeschooling. This isn't some temporary thing for me, Rachel. I want us to be a family. And I wanted to show you that we could do this and that Charlotte would be okay."

"Something tells me that she's going to be better than okay. And I want us to be a family, too. Wherever we end up."

"We'll have such fun coming back to the island for visits, too," Nicholas reminded her. "Adventure is always so much sweeter when you know there's a home waiting for you to come back to when you're ready for it. Plus, there are all kinds of requirements about meeting with teaching professionals and making sure Charlotte's schooling is running smoothly."

Rachel was so overwhelmed with love for him that she gave him another kiss, a slow and deep one this time. Whatever happened out there in the world, whatever places they visited, whatever adventures they had, they would do it together and love every moment of it.

"Let's get out of here." Rachel smiled, as happy as she'd ever been as she hugged both her daughter and the man she loved close to her. "The three of us have places to go."

EPILOGUE

It wasn't easy to organize a big bon voyage party in such a small amount of time, but fortunately, Paige was used to putting together large productions at the dance studio. At least this one didn't require choreography for thirty students.

Then again, from the way Morgan was looking at her...

"It's not going to happen," Paige told her sister.

"Oh, why not?" Morgan pouted. "Just one small dance number in the middle of the going-away party would be so much fun."

"You know I won't be able to get any students to help out on such short notice."

"Then why don't you do it? You're such a great dancer, Paige. You'd knock everyone's socks off—and Nicholas has never seen you dance before."

But Morgan knew that Paige didn't do the limelight. She never had. She could make anyone look good on stage, but she avoided the spotlight like the plague. Besides, this party was all about Rachel, Nicholas and Charlotte. They might not be "shuffling off to Buffalo," but they were heading off on a trip that would take them a lot farther than that.

It was going to be so strange not having her little niece running around the dance studio. At least not until Christmas, when the three of them were due to come back from...where was it again? Australia, then Japan was what she'd heard most recently. Paige was sure that Emily was working on getting their complete itinerary written down so that she could call in the rescue teams if they didn't check in often enough. And she knew that Morgan would be keeping in touch with Nicholas just in case he needed any help with his new TV show.

Ah, TV. She had one sister directing for it, another starring in her own segment, and now a third who was in love with a guy who was very likely going to become a huge TV star in the next month or two.

She was thrilled that each of them was getting what they wanted in their lives. Still, the most exciting thing of all to Paige was that her sisters had found men they really loved and wanted to spend the rest of their lives with. Every time Hanna and Joel came over from Seattle, they seemed so happy together. Now that Morgan had fallen back in love with Brian, she seemed so content. And Rachel truly seemed like herself again for the first time in years, thanks to Nicholas.

Would Paige get a chance to meet someone someday? A man who would be happy with the kind of simple, comfortable life that she really wanted?

"Earth to Paige," Morgan said with a smile. "I've got filming to get to this afternoon, so I need you to tell me now whether I need to pick up anything for the party on the way back."

"I think we've got everything already, but if I think of anything else that we need, I'll get it," Paige assured her sister. "You should just concentrate on the segment you're filming today."

Morgan was so good in front of the cameras. So beautiful and sparkling. Doing makeovers on TV was the perfect job for her. Just like teaching dance was the perfect job for Paige. One where she got to stay comfortably in the background while helping others to shine.

"Oh, before I go," Morgan said, "I wanted to mention that Brian and I are going to an awards ceremony on Saturday night that my TV network is throwing. Why don't you come with us? I'll do your makeup and—"

Paige shook her head, though she gentled the refusal with a smile. "It sounds like fun, but I'll be working on Saturday night with a few of our advanced students on their audition pieces for the Academy in Seattle."

In any case, even if she had been free, she wasn't interested in meeting—and possibly dating—a big TV star. She would be far happier with a nice, regular guy. Someone sweet and funny, and who attracted as little attention as she did. Less, even.

Unlike Rachel, Paige could certainly never date anyone in the public eye. Not in a million years. All that fuss. The endless glare of gossip magazines and photographs. Always having to worry about saying and doing the right thing in front of the cameras. No, Paige was quite happy to leave the limelight to her sisters.

Hoping that she would have a little time to dance in the studio as soon as she finished hanging the colorful streamers for Rachel, Nicholas and Charlotte's going-away party, Paige got back to work, all thoughts of dating a TV star happily forgotten.

~ THE END ~

ABOUT THE AUTHOR

When New York Times and USA Today bestseller Lucy Kevin released her first novel, SEATTLE GIRL, it became an instant bestseller. All of her subsequent sweet contemporary romances have been hits with readers as well, including WHEN IT'S LOVE (A Walker Island Romance, Book 3) which debuted at #1. Having been called "One of the top writers in America" by The Washington Post, she recently launched the very romantic Walker Island series. Lucy also writes contemporary romances as Bella Andre and her incredibly popular series about The Sullivans have been #1 bestsellers around the world, with more than 4 million books sold so far! If not behind her computer, you can find her swimming, hiking or laughing with her husband and two children. For a complete listing of books, as well as excerpts, contests, and to connect with Lucy please visit www.LucyKevin.com.

Printed in Great Britain
by Amazon.co.uk, Ltd.,
Marston Gate.